Hail

No

Book 1 of The Hail Raisers

By

Lani Lynn Vale

**ISBN-13:
978-1976546341**

**ISBN-10:
1976546346**

Dedication

Why are dedications so fucking hard to write? Seriously, they're hard as hell. I'm sure by now, if you've made it through all 40+ of my books, you know that I've thanked my mom, mother in law, husband, kids, sister, my readers, and hell I even dedicated one to my father who I haven't spoken to in five years. I guess this one will have to go to my chickens. They were a rather large inspiration when I wrote this book. :P Hope y'all enjoy it!

Acknowledgements

Danielle Palumbo- thank you for reading and loving my books. I know you don't have to, but it means the world to me that you want to do this for me.

Golden Czermak- Thank you for giving me such beautiful photos to work with for my covers.

Jake Wilson- Three years ago, when I stepped into this world, you were the one model that I always wanted on a cover. Now I have you on three. I can't tell you how freakin' awesome that is for me.

Kellie Montgomery- my editor that always seems to work me in when I give her zero notice. You're the best!

CONTENTS

Lani Lynn Vale

Vodka On The Rocks

Bad Apple

Dirty Mother

Rusty Nail

The Kilgore Fire Series

Shock Advised

Flash Point

Oxygen Deprived

Controlled Burn

Put Out

I Like Big Dragons Series

I Like Big Dragons and I Cannot Lie

Dragons Need Love, Too

Oh, My Dragon

The Dixie Warden Rejects

Beard Mode

Fear the Beard

Son of a Beard

I'm Only Here for the Beard

The Beard Made Me Do It

Beard Up

For the Love of Beard

There's No Crying in Baseball
Pitch Please

The Hail Raisers
Hail No

PROLOGUE

My level of sarcasm has gotten to the point where even I don't know whether I'm kidding or not.
-T-shirt

Evander

"Evander Lennox?"

I stood up, hating the way my knees creaked and popped.

I'd been in the military for seven years, then had worked for Hail for five more. It took spending four years in the pen, though, for me to start feeling fucking old.

I guess getting jumped in the dark would do that to a person.

"Hurry up, I don't have all day."

I gritted my teeth, but kept my pace deliberately slow.

Fuck him.

The parole officer, my parole officer, sent me a glare the moment I got to him.

"I don't need your bad attitude. I have your file in my office and I've spent the morning going over it. There won't be any 'accidents' while you're under my supervision, got it?"

The accidents he was referring to weren't accidents. I'd never said they were accidents.

In fact, I made sure to tell the guards exactly what had happened each time I'd had to use my hands to defend myself.

I was just lucky that the guards liked me and lied when they went to write their reports.

"Yes, Sir," I found myself choking out.

I wanted to call this man 'Sir' about as much as I wanted to take a shit in a plastic bag and carry it around in my pocket.

Thirty minutes later, I was leaving his office with a slew of rules that I now had to follow, as well as some regulations I wasn't aware that would be required of me when I'd started the day.

Needless to say, as I made my way home—walking, might I add— I wasn't in a good mood.

Not at fucking all.

***

I ripped the sheet off of the couch, and coughed when a cloud of dust filled the still, stagnant air around me.

"Fuck," I gasped, waving my hand in front of my face to clear the air.

It didn't work, but at least I'd given it the good old college try.

No one had been in here since I'd gone to prison. Not my friends. Not my dad—not that he even knew I'd gone to prison since I hadn't seen him in years, and that was *before* I'd done time. Not even my sister had bothered to come in here and clean up. Though, that didn't surprise me much. Every single one of my family members were selfish. I doubted cleaning my place up for me had even crossed their mind.

Yet, had they been there, it wouldn't have mattered. When I walked onto my property less than twenty minutes ago, I'd found not just overgrown weeds, but also trash. Junk. Old fucking tires.

It was as if my entire front yard was being used as the city dump while I was gone, and not one single person had done a damn thing to stop it.

Angry all over again, the next five minutes entailed me ripping sheets off of furniture and opening the windows in order to let the stale air out and the crisp, early October air in.

I threw the last of the sheets that were covering my furniture outside the door, and left the screen door propped open, allowing much needed air to permeate the room behind me.

"You need any help?"

I looked up to find Travis, the co-owner of Hail Auto Recovery, standing at my doorstep.

"Not really," I admitted. "I'm here now. That was the hard part."

It was.

I'd expected my sister to pick me up, but she never showed.

Not that that really surprised me, either.

My sister, yet again, was a selfish person. If it didn't benefit her in some way, she wouldn't do it.

"You didn't have a ride?"

I shrugged. "No."

"Why didn't you call me?" he asked.

I looked over at him.

"I called Dante. Didn't answer," I informed him. "I took that as the universal sign to fuck off."

He laughed humorlessly under his breath. "There's a lot of shit going down with Dante," he admitted. "And I'll tell you about it when there's a lot of whiskey to share. Until then, I brought you the keys to the truck."

My brows went up.

"Isn't it company policy not to hire men who've had a record?"

He looked at me like he wanted to smack me.

I shrugged. "Just sayin'."

He sighed.

"We both know you were dealt a bad hand," he said, tossing me a set of keys. "If you need any help, don't hesitate to ask. Use the truck. Don't use the truck. I don't fuckin' care. Just make sure you log personal and business miles so we can keep a record of them, okay?"

I nodded mutely, suddenly finding it hard to breathe.

They trusted me. They believed in me.

They'd been there the day I went down, and Travis was there the day I got out.

You find out who your friends are.

"Thank you," I said. "Do you…"

I hesitated, and he filled in the blanks.

"Do I know what happened to the horses?"

I nodded.

"They're at the old Mills farm off of sixty-nine. Mills knows you're back. He said he'd bring them back within the next week." He stepped away. "Your dog, I believe, is still at Civil's."

My eyes closed.

"Thanks, man."

Travis gave me a small salute, and then took off without another word.

I walked to the front door and watched him walk down the driveway and then blinked at the sight of him getting into a truck with a pretty blonde.

She looked cute, really cute. Definitely not his type, but there were a lot of changes that could happen in four years.

Apparently, Travis doing cute, bubbly blondes was one of them.

I watched the truck disappear down the road and then turned my attention back to the tow truck he'd left me.

It was brand-fucking-new.

There was no doubt in my mind that they just got it.

Why had he trusted me with something so fucking new?

I tossed the keys up into the air, took one more look around, and then walked to my bedroom and stepped up to the safe.

Once I entered the six-digit combination, I opened it, retrieved some cash, and then stared.

All my guns were there. The same exact place that they'd been in when I'd last closed it four years ago.

I'd have to get rid of them.

Just like the assholes who'd put me away, I was dealing with a probation officer who was a douche and a half, too. I could tell from the moment I met with him this morning that he wasn't going to be my favorite person.

Not at all.

I had eighteen more months on probation before I was finally a free man, and until then, I couldn't have any fuckin' alcohol, or firearms, within my vicinity.

I wouldn't sell them, no. I'd just lock them up somewhere and have someone else watch over them for a while.

Lifting my hand, I trailed my fingers down the barrel of my .45 that I used to carry concealed and felt a wave of unease trail over my skin.

How would I work without the ability to protect myself?

The auto recovery business was a dangerous one, and there wasn't a single time that I repossessed a truck or a car that it didn't have at least one hitch in the road.

With my brain in a weird sort of haze, I walked out of the house and to the tow truck.

Normally, I wouldn't have taken it so early but I had to go pick up Gertie.

I missed that dog like crazy, and it was him who I hated leaving behind the most.

I hoped he still remembered me.

Turns out I needn't have worried.

The minute that I arrived at Civil's, the one and only vet in town, it was to find a receptionist at the front desk that I'd never seen before.

Along with the town growing while I was away, apparently so did the vet clinic.

No longer was it a small, quaint clinic. Now it was an ungodly huge, likely multi-million-dollar clinic that looked like a fucking office building instead of a vet.

But whatever.

I didn't care.

As long as they kept Gertie safe.

"Can I help you?" the receptionist, a woman in her twenties who looked like she was way too dressed up to be working in a vet's office, asked sweetly.

Too sweet, if you asked me.

"I'm here to pick up my dog," I said. "Can I talk to Civil?"

The woman tilted her head.

"Civil is no longer with us," she said. "He passed away last fall. His daughter, however, is. She's in with a patient now, though."

My stomach tightened. "I'm sorry to hear that. Is that what's up with the new remodel?"

She nodded. "When Layne took over, she decided that a revamp was needed."

I looked around the place.

I didn't see anything wrong with the old one, but apparently, this new vet did.

Pity.

"Do you think when she's done with the patient that she will talk to me?" I asked. "I won't take long."

I just hoped that Civil had held true to his word and had this woman look after my dog just as well as Civil did.

"Yes," she agreed. "I'll have her do that when she's done."

I nodded. "Thank you."

A deep bark from the other room had me turning to stare at the closed door.

I knew that bark.

Everything inside of me wanted to go to that door and throw it open, but I didn't.

My guess was that Gertie knew I was there, too.

He'd always been able to tell; I didn't expect now to be any different.

I took a seat next to the magazine rack and picked up the first thing I saw, which was a magazine about chickens, and wondered idly if they were hard to care for.

I'd always wanted chickens, but I had never gotten around to getting any, thankfully.

I'd made it to the fifth page, which was talking about egg incubation and how to hatch your own eggs at home, when my name was called.

"Mr. Lennox?"

I looked up to find a woman dressed in scrubs, with blonde hair pulled into a tight pony-tail on the top of her head, staring at me expectantly.

I offered her my hand, which she took and leg go almost as if she was scared to touch me.

"How can I help you?"

"I'm here to pick up my dog."

She frowned. "Which dog?"

"My German Shepherd. He's been here for a while. I left him with your dad, actually. Gertie."

Her face completely closed down.

"You can't have him," she said plainly.

I tilted my head. "What do you mean I can't have him?"

"He's been here for four years," she replied. "He's my dog now."

The bones in my jaw started to creak.

"I paid for four and a half years of boarding before I left. That's over ten grand. I know that it's been four years. I didn't have any choice about going away, unfortunately. Civil said he'd take care of him for me. He wasn't boarded. He was taken to his home. And he also took care of my horses at my friend's place."

She sniffed at me. "I know. I was the one taking care of him."

I crossed my arms over my chest.

"I appreciate everything that you did, but now that I'm back, I'd like to take him home."

I could see by the stubborn set of her jaw that she wasn't going to give him to me.

"No."

My stomach started to tighten as anger started to swirl through my veins.

"How about you bring Gertie out here, and we see who exactly he wants to go to?" I semi-snapped.

I knew who Gertie would choose.

The dog was barking up a storm now, and I could tell that if he were let out, he wouldn't want anything to do with the woman.

I didn't care who she was, or what she'd done for me the last four years. I'd paid her father, and in turn, the vet. I had a fucking contract in my back pocket. Which I gave her next.

She took it with a look of disgust on her face.

"What is this supposed to be?"

A guarantee that this very thing wouldn't happen.

"A contract between this clinic and me," I explained. "That they would watch my dog for four years, while I was in prison, and that when I got out, he'd be given back to me."

"We don't do this," she snapped.

I laughed. "Your father did it. And it was signed by both him and me. Him for his business, Civil Veterinary, and me, the dog's owner. Trust me when I say, you won't win this one."

She hissed out a breath.

"How about you let him choose," she snapped.

I laughed.

"There's loyalty, and then there's destiny, ma'am. Gertie was mine from when he was a year old, until we both retired from the Marines together when he was five years old," I informed her. "We saved each others' lives countless times, and I've never spent a day away from him, intentionally, since he was given to me."

She pursed her lips.

"I've fed him for the last four years. He's slept in my house," she countered back. "I've cared for him, and ownership is nine tenths of the law."

I laughed at her.

"Ma'am, with all due respect, ownership ain't shit," I countered. "You can refuse to give him to me now, but I can guarantee that the first chance he gets, he'll leave your house and come straight to mine now that he knows I'm back."

She looked at me like she didn't believe me.

"He's a dog. He won't know better," she informed me.

"You hear him goin' crazy?" I asked.

We both did.

The moment that he'd heard my voice, he'd started going fucking nuts. Scratching, throwing himself against the wall. Anything that would help him get out there, he'd do, until he was back with me.

That was the kind of friendship we had.

I'd pulled him out of a pile of rubble when a building had collapsed on him. He'd saved me from taking a sniper's bullet to the eye.

And those were only two examples of the many times we'd been there for each other.

Time and distance were nothing compared to the bond we shared.

I didn't care if it'd been eight years.

You didn't forget a bond like that.

"Go get him," I ordered her.

She shook her head. "I'm not giving him back to a criminal. You can call your lawyer…"

But she forgot about her staff who were in the same building as her, and when they heard the commotion, they came out of the very door that Gertie was practically tearing down, just to see what was wrong.

The moment he was set free, he vaulted over the counter and sped toward me like a speeding bullet.

Gertie was a huge German Shepherd. He was nearly a hundred and twenty pounds, and he was also the size of a small Great Dane.

The moment he got to me, he launched himself at me, and I could do nothing but catch him and wrap my arms around him like he was a person.

His whimpering, as well as his excitement, was enough to cause tears to spring to my eyes.

"God, Gert," I groaned. "I've missed you so much."

He was literally shaking with excitement in my arms, and I closed my eyes, burying my face into the scruff of his neck like I'd done so many times before.

"Gertie, heel."

Gertie didn't even react to the woman's voice, and I chose to leave without saying another thing to her.

"This isn't over!"

I ignored that, too.

It was over, whether she wanted to admit it or not.

Not only was Gertie obviously saying that he was mine, but I also now had possession of him.

There was not a damn thing in the world she could do about it.

CHAPTER 1

Beware of chickens. They can be real peckers.
-Wall sign

Kennedy

Three months later

The city of Hostel, Texas was hopping.

We weren't in New Orleans, but we were in a town that celebrated the holiday just as hard as New Orleans did, though to a much smaller scale due to the town's size. When it was time for Mardi Gras, we went from a quaint little farming town with barely any excitement to crazy extremes.

Beginning in early January through Fat Tuesday, it was a nonstop party.

Today was no different.

With Mardi Gras only a few days away, Hostel was in full party prep mode.

Even the feed store—one of the few places in town besides the library, the Wal-Mart, and the burger joint that I practically lived at—was celebrating.

I loaded one more bag of feed onto my flatbed cart, and then rolled it up to the register, very conscious of how difficult the cart was to stop.

In fact, I was concentrating so intently on the progression of my load that I didn't see the other cart coming from the aisle beside me until I was lying flat on the floor, my flatbed cart now four feet in front of me and not stopping.

I groaned and pushed myself up to a sitting position, and then looked at the cart that was pushed into my path.

It was manned by a child. A four or five-year-old at most.

I grimaced and looked away from the little boy just in time to see my very heavy cart, loaded down with four bags of chicken feed and two bags of all-feed, smack straight into the back of a man's legs.

He cursed and whipped his head around to look at the offending object, only to turn his eyes even further toward me.

The moment that those eyes, steel blue and so intense, landed on me, the little breath I'd been able to catch left my body in an audible whoosh.

"You okay?"

I blinked.

Then nodded, not trusting myself to say a word.

He held his finger up to the cashier and walked toward me, shooting the kid, who was trying to move forward with his cart despite me still being in his path, a glare before offering me his hand.

He had tattoos on his knuckles.

Actually, he had tattoos on his arm that extended to his knuckles, but still, he had tattoos on his knuckles.

I took the hand.

Mine so white compared to his tanned and tattooed one.

Effortlessly he lifted me to my feet and stared at me.

"You have a cut," he pointed to my jaw, or somewhere near it since I couldn't quite see.

Then he pulled out a fucking handkerchief from his pocket and pressed it against my face.

I brought my hand up and placed it on the handkerchief, which happened to still be in his hand, and said, "Thank you."

My words were so low that even I barely heard them, but he did and nodded as he stepped back.

When the kid tried to hit us with his cart again, and the man whipped his head to the side and growled, "Stop that."

The kid froze, and a woman who'd obviously not been paying attention to her child said, "Evander, I'm so sorry!"

The man turned to her.

"Your son just knocked this woman flat on her ass," he said none too gently. "Watch that kid of yours."

The woman flushed and looked at me guiltily, but not because she felt bad. It was obvious that she didn't care if her child knocked me down or not. What she cared about was that this Evander had made her look bad in front of the entire feed store.

"I'm sorry," she lied.

I shrugged. "It's okay. Are you okay?"

Evander looked at me, then nodded. "Fine."

Then he walked away, finally giving me the chance to take him in fully.

He was tall with jet black hair that was clipped closely to his scalp. He had to be at least six-foot-five or six. He had on a black t-shirt that had Hail Auto Recovery written on it and was so tight that I could see every single dip and indention that his muscles made beneath the shirt. He had on dark washed blue jeans that looked stained and dirty from a day full of work, and he had black motorcycle boots that looked damn near as worn out as the pants covering his large feet.

Then there were the tattoos.

And there were a lot of them.

From underneath his t-shirt all the way down to his hands. They were even on the palms of his hands. It was more than obvious that the man liked his ink.

The cart hit me in the ankles again, and I jumped in surprise, then shot the kid a glare.

"Ouch."

The mother snorted. "Honey, he's out of your league."

Then she pulled the cart back and started back to the boots she'd been checking out, completely shutting me out.

Rolling my eyes at her words, I started toward where my cart was now stopped directly next to the register, and listened to the man behind the checkout counter and Evander speaking.

"I need a three-hundred-and-forty-foot roll of goat wire fence, eighty t-posts, and some tie wire," Evander murmured. "I also have an ag exemption."

The boy started clicking away at his computer, but my eyes were only for the man who was now looking out the front window.

"Okay, that'll be four hundred and sixty-two dollars and thirty-two cents," the boy hesitated. "Please sign for the ag exemption."

Evander did, and I watched the way his muscled forearm bunched as he wrote his name. In perfect cursive.

Who the hell could write that pretty on those little stupid screens?

I knew I couldn't. Those things were the devil, and it never failed that my cursive would end up looking like someone else's name that wasn't mine.

"If you'll take the receipt to the side gate, someone will load you…"

Evander suddenly darted outside, leaving his receipt.

I watched him go, then turned back to the checker, who was also watching Evander go.

"I'll give it to him on my way out," I said. "He's parked right next to me."

I'd, of course, seen the tow truck as I'd parked my old Ford Diesel next to it. It was beautiful—big, black, and shiny with skulls and crossbones painted across the hood. The airbrushed words, Hail Auto Recovery, were even prettier.

It had to be new, probably even brand new.

I'd have driven the hell out of that truck.

"Okay," the checker shrugged. "That all you have today?"

I nodded. "Yep. Until next week."

He chuckled and rang me up. After I signed for my own ag exemption, I pocketed both receipts and started outside, only to stop when I saw the tow truck moved and now backing up to a car that was so shiny and beautiful that I'd be scared to even walk next to it for fear of scratching it on my way inside the store.

I knew it was a sports car, but beyond that, I didn't know exactly what kind it was. But it looked expensive…and it was now being towed by the biggest, meanest looking motherfucker on the planet.

There was a small man dressed in gym clothes—expensive ones that matched and were in bright, obnoxious colors—talking to

Evander, but Evander kept loading the car up without saying a word.

Then the little man tried to touch Evander, and Evander shoved him away so brutally that I winced.

The guy hit the pavement with a crash, but he was up again and got even further into Evander's face within seconds.

I bit my lip, watching as the two fought it out.

Evander only thwarting the little man's attempts to touch the controls that were on the side of the tow truck.

Then the car was lifted into the air by the huge boom thing hanging at the back of the truck, and the little guy started to scream at the top of his lungs like a six-year-old girl—a kind of high-pitched squeal that hurt my ears even from all the way across the parking lot.

A crowd had gathered outside the feed store's front entrance as everyone started to come outside to watch.

The occupants from the other buildings—a cake shop, the gym that it was likely the little man had come from, and a restaurant just a little down from the gym—came outside as well and gawked at the spectacle.

"Man, I don't know why you didn't pay your bills, but I'm only doing my job. If you want it back, you'll have to get your payments current."

"Can I at least get my stuff?"

The little guy panted, no longer screaming.

He must've seen the reality of the situation, because he looked defeated.

"No. But if you want to come by Hail, then you can get your shit there from the office lady," Evander grunted. "Have a good day."

The man backed up as Evander started to round his truck, and then went back to the gym.

"Asshole," the guy muttered.

I didn't agree. Evander hadn't been an asshole. He'd been doing his job.

However, I suppose if that was me that that had happened to, I probably would have been thinking the same thing.

Regardless, I stepped out into the parking lot and started toward him.

"Umm, Evander?"

Evander looked up from where he'd been getting into his truck.

"Yeah?" he questioned.

"You forgot your receipt," I said, handing it to him over the door that separated us.

He took it, then nodded his head in thanks.

"Have a good one."

I nodded back, backed my cart up, and moved two rows over and down to where my old Ford truck was parked, and dropped the tailgate.

I grunted when I picked up my first bag, thinking that I was getting more and more tired as the day wore on.

It was now two in the afternoon, and I'd been working since five this morning. Plus, I hadn't eaten.

Maybe a burger from Maple's was what I'd do. It was quick and it sounded really good. And it was in the same parking lot as the bank, where I had to go to next.

I'd just reached down for the second bag when a set of tattooed hands filled my vision.

"I got it," Evander said, picking up two bags at a time.

That was a hundred pounds, and he'd lifted it like it was effortless.

"T-thank you," I stumbled over my words.

Evander reached down for the rest of the bags and then tossed them into the truck bed before closing the tailgate.

And without another word, he was gone.

Shaking my head, I got into my old truck and started it up, praying to sweet baby Jesus that it started without backfiring.

I'd made it all the way out of town, and was pulling into my driveway, when I realized that I hadn't stopped for the burger that I'd been craving.

Groaning, I pulled over to the side of the driveway and contemplated what to do.

I had eggs—I always had eggs, though—and I thought I might have some bacon. I could make myself some, but my mind was set on a really juicy burger, and it wasn't going to settle for anything less.

Which had me pulling the old truck into the driveway, and turning around.

Only, just when I was about to pull out of the driveway, I remembered that I was planning on taking my father's old 'Cuda out for a drive to keep the battery up.

Knowing that if I didn't do it today, it'd be next week before I could do it due to previous obligations including meeting my sister, Trixie for her doctor's appointment tomorrow at two, I decided to go ahead and do it now.

Plus, it didn't hurt that tonight was classic car night at the Dairy Queen.

Not that I would be going there. However, since the antique license plates my Pop had on the car had stipulations—such as you couldn't drive it unless it was to a car show or to do regular maintenance on the vehicle at a mechanic's shop—it was best to have a good excuse for why you were taking it out, despite knowing that you weren't doing anything wrong.

Though, cops always made me nervous when I was in the 'Cuda.

My father had kept that 'Cuda in perfect condition, and there wasn't much in this world that would catch a cop's eye faster than a car painted cherry red with white racing stripes. Well, that and the fact that it had a 383 big block in it.

With my plan firmly in place—IE, getting into the car and driving to get myself that burger I'd been craving without getting pulled over by the cops—I headed out, being sure to keep the GPS on the front window where I could see it.

This car's speedometer didn't work. The gas tank also didn't work once you got below a half tank, and I wasn't even going to mention the fact that the ignition was long past overdue to be replaced.

Apparently, old cars were notorious for being able to start without a key, due to the ignition fucking up somehow, but I hadn't known it until my dad had passed the car into my care once he'd injured himself on a tractor.

That, by no means, meant it was mine. It just meant that I was charged with taking care of it, and making sure that if he ever was in need of the car, it'd be in driving condition.

Once I was on the way to the burger joint, Maple's, I started humming to myself, wondering if everyone in my family was cursed.

My mother had died of ovarian cancer. My older sister, Heidi, had died of breast cancer. My dad had fallen off a tractor while tilling the fields to get them ready for planting and was paralyzed from the waist down. My brother, Paul, was run off the road by a drunk driver, and as a result, he now had such debilitating back and leg problems that he couldn't work because he couldn't stand.

Then there was my sister, Trixie.

Trixie was the baby, though not by much.

She was my twin sister. I was older by four minutes, but you wouldn't know it. Trixie was a natural mother hen. She always wanted to make sure everyone else was okay before she did anything for herself, and I hadn't been spared from her care.

Now, it was my turn to watch over her, and I wasn't looking forward to it.

Not because I wasn't willing to take care of her, but because I didn't like the idea of her being unwell enough to need watching over.

I pulled into the parking lot of Maple's on auto-pilot, barely registering the fact that the parking lot was full before I parked and started inside.

I walked past a gaggle of men who'd been busy looking at the antique car in the next parking lot, and nodded my head at the men when they said, 'nice ride.'

I wasn't paying attention to where I was going, so when I face planted into something that felt very similar to a human wall, I squeaked in surprise and started to fall backwards.

"Sorry, Sweetheart."

I looked up at hearing that slow, Southern drawl, and blinked in surprise.

"Wow," I managed to say. "That sure did hurt."

Please, kill me now.

He offered me his hand, and I reluctantly took it. "Thank you, Mr. Evander."

Evander blinked. "Van is fine."

I nodded. "Here for a burger?"

Then I mentally kicked myself in the shin. Are you fucking kidding, Kennedy? This is the best burger place in not only Hostel but also the surrounding counties!

There was only one thing that you could get at Maple's and that was a hamburger—unless you counted the complimentary beans that Maple herself cooked in the kitchen every day from scratch.

"Yeah," he agreed. "Hungry."

Of course, he was.

Jesus Christ, Kennedy. You're so fucking weird.

"Righty-O," I called, maneuvering myself around him where he still stood in the doorway, holding the door for me to enter. "Have a good one."

Righty-O? Are you here for a burger?

Jesus.

Sidling up to the far end of the counter, I waited behind a few other customers for the line to move and watched the woman ahead of me instead of turning my head to examine the man that was standing at my back.

He had his large, tattooed arms stretched out across his chest, and he was looking at me.

I could tell.

I felt it on the back of my neck like a physical caress against my skin.

But he didn't say a word, and neither did I.

And by the time I'd gotten up to the counter, another register had opened, and he'd moved to that line and ordered at the same time as me.

"No pickles," I said to the lady just as Evander said, "Extra pickles."

I grinned at him, but he didn't look at me, his eyes studying the menu.

"I'd also like some chili cheese fries," I said to the lady.

"You realize that those are made for two, right?" the young teen asked.

I nodded. "Yes, but since you don't put that on the smaller order, I have to order the big order."

She grunted something, and I had to catch the urge to roll my eyes.

She was a teenager. From the look she'd just given me, you'd have thought I'd given her a grave insult that she could never recover from.

Once I had my little buzzer, a cup filled to the brim with ice water and a bowl of beans, I took a seat at the one and only empty spot in the entire room and started to shovel them down.

Which was why I didn't see the man—Evander—looking around the room with open curiosity to where he'd sit until he was standing right next to me.

"You mind if I share the end of your table?"

I looked down the length of the eight-person table, and then shook my head. "No, go right ahead."

He took a seat at the opposite end, and started to shovel his own beans into his mouth, leaving me to wonder if I should bother to make small talk or just ignore him and act like he wasn't sitting at my table.

I chose option two, and started to eat my beans while also wondering if this place knew that their lighting was shit. The acoustics weren't all that great, either, making it almost impossible to hear anything from someone that was already directly next to you.

The same old men that I always saw at the coffee shop in the mornings were now crowding up the middle of the restaurant. Their laughter was on the verge of being too loud, but with nothing to control their exuberance—IE, their wives—they talked and joked and were having a merry old time.

Until they weren't, and that had a lot to do with their numbers being called and their burgers being ready.

I was so engrossed watching the men get up to put the fixings on their food when the man from the opposite side of the table gestured to me with empty hands.

"Can you pass the salt?"

I reached for the salt and the pepper, handing them both to him.

"I asked for the salt," he repeated himself.

"Okay," I mumbled. "You got the salt."

He held up the pepper.

I shrugged. "My father says that if you don't pass the salt and the pepper together, you lose your girlfriend."

He blinked, then blinked again.

"W-what?" he stuttered, sounding utterly confused.

I nodded soberly. "I'm not sure if you actually lose your girlfriend," I babbled. "But I've done because it makes my family laugh. Even my brother did it. My sister. Her husband. Their children. I think at this point, it's just a habit."

He muttered something under his breath.

"I see that." He used the salt and pushed it back to me, then pushed the pepper down a moment later.

"You just lost your girlfriend," I informed him, a smile on my face.

He grunted. "That might be why I don't have a fuckin' girlfriend."

I don't know why hearing that news made me so blessedly happy, but it did. However, I chose not to comment when it was clear that he didn't want to speak.

Both of our orders were called at the same time, and he got up and brought both back to the table before I could so much as stand from my chair.

So, there I sat, enjoying my burger, while I tried not to stare.

It worked.

At least for a little while.

"Napkin?"

I handed him a napkin, then decided to be proactive.

"Anything else? Steak sauce?"

I never understood steak sauce at a burger joint, especially one with burgers that tasted as good as Maple's did. Nonetheless, it was there so I thought I'd offer it.

He shook his head and reached for multiple napkins, laying them out on the table before taking his bun off.

Then, before my eyes, he blotted his burger with the napkins, and then proceeded to do it again and again until there was no more grease to be soaked up off the burger.

So that had been why he'd had all of his condiments, mustard and ketchup included, put off to the side.

He quickly reassembled his burger, putting back first the onions, then the cheese, followed by the mustard, pickles, and then the ketchup.

Once everything was piled high, he shoved the bun on and squished it down so that mustard and ketchup squirted out the sides.

"Are you new around here?"

His eyes, those beautiful steel blue ones that were quickly starting to be my favorite color, turned to me.

"No," he grunted. "I went away for a while, but I'm back now."

I wanted to ask him more questions, but he shoved his face full of French fries and turned his face away so that he was staring at his tray and nothing else.

He ate fast.

So fast, in fact, that I was only through half my burger and only some of my fries when he was collecting his trash and standing to go.

"See you around," I called to him.

He glanced down at me, shook his head, and then walked away without another word.

Rude!

Lani Lynn Vale

CHAPTER 2

I'm a simple woman. I like handsome, muscled, tattooed men with beards and donuts.
-Kennedy's secret thoughts

Kennedy

I hoped that whatever news that we got today, that it wasn't something detrimental.

But it has to be, my sister's words from earlier still rang in my ears *Why else would the doctor call me into his office if it wasn't bad?*

The other question was what if there was something seriously wrong with her? How the hell were they going to pay for it? She and I came from a family of farmers. Her husband was a fourth-generation farmer. There'd been a drought this year, and honestly, I was halfway convinced that they didn't even have health insurance.

Not to mention they had four young kids.

And it wasn't like I could help.

I was a farmer, too. I lived off my craft. I lived simply. I had insurance…what I did not have was insurance that was very good. I had the bronze plan—the lowest of the low.

But at least I had insurance…

Oh, God. This was going to be horrible.

"Are you ready, Freddy?" I asked my sister.

She turned her haunted eyes to me.

"Yeah," she mumbled.

I offered her my hand, and we walked, holding on to each other into the hospital.

***

Shock resonated through me at hearing the doctor's words.

"I have what?" my sister gasped.

The doctor looked at her with pity-filled eyes.

"Ovarian cancer," he repeated. "Stage three."

I looked around the room.

She'd gone to the doctor for a routine physical for work. Now we were here today facing a nightmare.

"What now?" I finally settled on, noticing that my sister was too surprised to talk.

"Now, you fight."

"I didn't want to fight. I wanted to live my life. I wanted to go to work and spend time with my family and friends. I wanted to freakin' live!"

Fighting meant a whole lot of pain, and since she was a nurse— though she hadn't worked in well over six years—she knew more than most.

Hell, even I knew that the debilitating pain that lay ahead for her. I knew that she'd wake up most days and not feel like getting out of bed.

I'd already witnessed our sister, and mother going through their own battles with cancer.

I knew that this was going to be tough.

So tough.

"Why not just take her ovaries?"

"No!" came my sister's vehement denial.

"That would be why," the doctor said. "When her endometriosis acted up, and I suggested having a hysterectomy, she refused. I knew that wasn't something she'd want to do unless there was no other possible way to avoid it."

I looked over at my sister.

"Trix," I said carefully. "I realize that you want more kids, but…"

"I said no!"

Right.

"We're going to run with this, Trixie. You don't have time to waste."

She didn't have time to waste.

Right.

"I'll expect you to start chemo on Monday," he said. "I'm referring you to a doctor the next floor up." He gestured with his hand. "Today. You have an appointment right after this one," he sighed. "This is bad, yes, but it's not completely the end of the world."

Not the end of the world.

Right.

"Head on over there now. They're expecting you."

***

"If I'm being honest here, I realize that the best option would be to take the ovaries…"

The oncologist tried again.

I'd tried in the elevator. Hell, I was sure that her husband would try, too.

"Can I still go on our cruise?" she questioned. "It's next week."

He nodded, but I could tell that he wanted to start treatment right this second. Today, if possible.

"Yes, you can go as long as you feel up to it." He stood up. "With your permission, we'll schedule the procedure to implant your medical access port for tomorrow or the next day. Do you have any questions about that?"

He didn't need to explain what that was or where it was going—at least not to me.

My brother had had one. My mom. My sister.

My stomach hurt.

My head was pounding, and I wanted nothing more than to crawl into a corner and cry.

But I wouldn't.

Not in front of Trixie.

"No," she cleared her throat. "That'll be fine."

He nodded soberly. "All right. Millie, my nurse, will be outside waiting to take some of your information down. Once we have you scheduled, you'll need to go into the hospital to register the day before. Now you can do that at any time, but I recommend you go either mid-afternoon or closer to closing time. They'll take a sample of your blood, just in case, and then get you all set-up and ready-to-go insurance wise. Anything else?"

She shook her head. "No."

He stood up and offered her his hand.

She took it, and shook it once before dropping it.

"We'll get through this," the doctor, Albertson his name badge said, promised. "I'll see you in a few days. Millie will also schedule your next few appointments, okay?"

Trixie continued to nod.

"Trixie…"

She shook her head. "Let's get this scheduled, and then you can take me home. I need to talk to Darren."

I did as she asked, and the entire way down the elevator, out into the parking lot and to her house, she never said a word.

When I pulled up in front of her house, it was to see her youngest running toward us, a look of utter glee on his face to see that his mother was home.

"Thank you," she whispered. "Can you come pick DJ up in an hour and take him to baseball practice?"

I nodded mutely, not trusting myself to speak.

Then she was gone, picking Jaxon up into the air and spinning him around, a happy smile on her face.

I continued to watch for a little longer, smiling slightly when Darren came out of the house and looped a muscular arm around her shoulders.

The moment they started talking, I pulled out of their driveway, and made it about halfway down the street before I couldn't help it anymore, and started to cry.

Maybe if I just sat here for an hour and cried, then I could go pick him up and not have to drive all the way home.

With my master plan written, I shoved the door open and nearly fell out, bringing my hands up to my head and trying to breathe through the pain.

It didn't help, so I started to walk.

CHAPTER 3

I wish I could copy and paste you into my bed.
-Not a good pick-up line

Evander

"Hello?" I answered, looking at my watch to see if I'd have enough time to hit the grocery store before I had to go pick up Dalton.

Dalton was my sister's stepson, and a complete and utter asshole to anyone who wasn't his father.

But, like the total sucker that I was for my sister, even though she treated me like shit, I'd offered to pick him up and take him to baseball practice despite not really liking the kid all that much.

I'd missed a lot, being gone for the last four years, and one of those things was my sister's remarriage to a man I wasn't sure I liked.

Not with the way he allowed his kid to treat my sister like a total piece of trash who wasn't good enough to make him food, let alone spend time in his house while his father was away at work.

Seriously, there was one person in this world who I'd do anything for—had done anything for—and that was my sister.

Sure, she never returned the favor, but I was her big brother. And no matter what she did and how she treated me, she'd always be my little sister.

If she wanted me to take her punk step-kid to the baseball park for practice, then I'd fuckin' do it. But I sure the fuck wouldn't enjoy it.

"I have an abandoned car for you to pick up," came the annoyed voice of the woman who worked in dispatch. "I tried to call the towing side, but they're all busy at a wreck on the interstate."

I sighed. "I'll pick it up, but I won't be delivering it to the yard until tomorrow morning. I have a baseball practice at six I have to take a kid to and that's in less than an hour."

"Thanks," Cindy's said, and then she hung up.

Rolling my eyes at the way she spent as little time talking to me as possible, I started the truck and pulled out of the grocery parking lot.

Guess those would be waiting until tomorrow, just like the rest of the fencing I'd yet to pick up from the feed store.

But, I had a busy life, and busy meant I couldn't get myself into trouble, thank God.

Hence the reason I didn't complain to Cindy like I would've done four years ago.

I didn't work for the towing side of the business, and she damn well knew it.

There were multiple people that she could've called, one of those being the motherfucker on call for the towing side, yet she'd called me.

That was likely more due to the fact that she was still irrationally angry with me for 'dumping' her.

I hadn't dumped her, though.

I'd gone to prison.

Sure, I guess I could've stayed with her, but no woman needed to wait four years on a man who was in jail.

Although, now that I had time to think about it, I knew that her loyalty hadn't been that great. It'd taken her all of a month to move on, thanks to the fact that she'd had what was left of my last paycheck to live on before she made any drastic decisions.

Not that we'd have made it much longer had I not gone to prison.

Cindy was a good girl, but she was too clingy.

Even now she called with some bullshit excuses just to see what I was doing even though I hadn't had to answer to her in well over four years.

Grumbling to myself, I turned down the street that was indicated to have an abandoned truck on it, and started to cruise down the road, hoping to find the truck and get it loaded up quickly before I had to be at the baseball practice.

After another two minutes of driving, I rounded a corner to find a familiar Ford sitting there, almost mocking me.

I hadn't been able to get the woman out of my thoughts since I'd seen her at the feed store.

Then when we'd sat next to each other at Maple's, that'd just been the icing on the cake.

Now, two days later, I was looking at her truck without her in it, and I started to get a *really* bad feeling about it.

I pulled over to the side of the road, directly in front of her truck so that we were nose to nose, and hopped out, my eyes scanning the immediate area.

What was her name? I hadn't actually thought to get it, and now more than ever I was kicking myself for that.

"Hey, girl!" I yelled out. "Are you okay?"

Hey girl? What was I, ten?

I called out again and again, until I finally started to think I was going to have to tow her truck because she wasn't actually there, but before I could head back to my own, branches snapped somewhere in the distance, drawing my eye.

I turned to face the woman as she came out of the woods.

She looked different.

Less put together, maybe.

When I'd seen her the day before, she'd been wearing these ridiculously tight leggings, a black t-shirt, and rain boots with chickens on them.

She'd looked fucking adorable with her hair up, and her face sun kissed. It was as if she'd just come in from a hard day of working outside. She even had a slight sheen of sweat on her face.

Today she was in something that was more formal. Black dress pants, a blue silk shirt, and low-slung heels.

Today, though, her smile—the one thing that'd drawn me in despite not wanting to be immersed in anything that had to do with a woman ever again—was missing.

"Hey, you okay?"

She looked up, looking almost surprised to see me, and frowned.

"What are you doing here?" she whispered, swiping at her eyes.

I continued to stare right at her.

"I'm here because there was a call about an abandoned vehicle," I gestured with my head to her truck. "Apparently, it was too close to the road for someone's liking."

She shook her head. "I'll move it."

I stopped her with a hand on her arm, or more like just my fingers.

I knew I shouldn't, but I did anyway.

"So, why did you pull over and start crying?"

She looked at me, and my breath hitched in my throat.

"My sister," she murmured after a while. "We found out that she has cancer."

My stomach sank.

"I'm sorry."

She shrugged. "I guess I shouldn't be surprised," she admitted. "My mom and older sister both died of it. It was only a matter of time before either she or I got it."

She sounded so lost and upset that I wanted to pull her into my arms, but I didn't.

It wouldn't do to let her be seen with the criminal—a man who was arrested for assault and then sentenced to four years in prison.

Yeah, it'd sucked. Big time.

Though, I wouldn't stop myself from carrying out that assault again—even though the one I'd been charged with hadn't been one that I'd committed.

What I would've done, however, was make sure that the asshole who doctored up the footage would've had that camera shoved up his ass instead of assuming that the little shit had even the slightest amount of morals in his slimy little body.

I stepped away from her. "See you around, Ma'am."

"Thank you," she murmured. "See you around."

Then she got into her truck and drove away, leaving me staring after her with worry starting to fill the pit of my belly.

***

An hour later, I'd just pulled the truck into the parking lot of the baseball fields, and pulled into a parking spot at the back, when the kid I was transporting grumbled something rude under his breath.

"What was that?" I asked.

"Can you park any further away?" Dalton snapped.

I narrowed my eyes.

"Probably," I muttered darkly. "But this is good for me. It's not for you?"

Dalton didn't say anything, lucky for him, and instead hopped out of the truck and yanked his bag with him.

The bat hit the metal of the truck, and I had to grit my teeth to keep from snapping at the little asshole.

"You know where you're going?"

Dalton didn't bother to reply. Instead, he shrugged his bag high over his shoulder and started stomping across the lot to the field.

I sighed, and started to close the door to the truck when I saw a familiar blue Ford pull into the parking lot, finding a much closer spot than I'd found, and park.

The familiar woman—looking much more comfortable now in a pair of jeans and a t-shirt, slipped down out of the truck and rounded the truck's bed, stopping at the side to open the door for a boy that resembled her.

Her son, maybe?

I started forward, trying not to look like I was staring, and made my way to the bleachers where I would reside for the next two hours of the boys' practice.

Which afforded me a great view of the woman—the woman whose name I still didn't know. At least not yet.

She took a seat three rows in front of me and kept her head straight ahead while she watched the little boy who'd gotten out of her truck.

She didn't yell and scream, though, like some of the other mothers.

She stayed facing straight ahead, she didn't speak to anyone, and she didn't even seem to notice when people spoke to her.

Left to her own devices, she stayed there practically unmoving as the sorrow I felt for her grew in my chest, leaving me to wonder if maybe I should try to talk to her.

"Evander!"

I turned at the sound of that voice and spotted the coach, who was staring at me.

"Would you mind throwing some balls to the boys?"

I grunted in reply, then stood up and made my way down the bleachers.

It wasn't until I was halfway down that I realized that the woman was watching me.

Her face was no longer filled with sorrow.

It was filled with curiosity.

"Hey," I mumbled on my way past.

She didn't say anything, she only nodded in reply.

And I sighed as I made my way to the dugout.

What did I care if she said anything to me, anyhow?

She was Trouble, with a capital T.

Lani Lynn Vale

CHAPTER 4

To be honest, I'd rather be drinking coffee on my unicorn instead of whatever this work business is.
-Kennedy's secret thoughts

Kennedy

"Is that Evander Lennox?"

I turned my head at one of the mother's whispered words.

"I think it is. When did he get out of prison?"

"Apparently, not too long ago. My husband is his parole officer."

That made me curious.

I'd been to enough of DJ's practices that I knew some of these mothers, and the one who'd spoken about her husband being the man's parole officer was none other than Maddison Jane, the biggest gossip among the entire group.

At the last practice I'd taken DJ to, she'd been the one who said that her kids weren't allowed to ride four wheelers because they were dangerous. But then she went on to say how her kids were taking horseback riding lessons to give them an 'eclectic' background.

If there was a picture next to stupidity in the dictionary, it would be of her.

"Wow, he's really put on some muscle since the last time I saw him," Edith, one of the other mothers, not-so-quietly whispered. "Do you think he has AIDS?"

I stiffened.

"I don't see him allowing anybody, inmates or not, to do anything to his butthole," Maddison said. "And I read his file while my husband wasn't looking. He lives back at his house now."

"That place on the Old Highway?" Edith asked. "That place was trashed over the last four years. Everybody used it as a dumping ground for all their unwanted shit. Nobody took care of it at all."

My brows furrowed.

I didn't remember any houses on the Old Highway but one, and if that was Evander's house, and this town didn't treat it well, I would be so pissed.

I'd been in Hostel, Texas for all of three and a half years. Though, my father had been here a lot longer than that. As had my sister.

Me, I'd only gotten here after my mother decided to tell me about my father. They'd had a weird sort of relationship when we were younger.

Mom and Dad had met and fallen in love. Then, four years into their marriage, it'd fallen apart. However, my mom had been pregnant with me and my sister at the time, and they'd stayed together long enough to split their kids up right down the middle.

My mother got the oldest of the four children and the youngest—me. My father got the other two.

Then they never spoke to each other, or of each other, ever again. If we tried, it was shut down. The consequences—IE my mother freaking the fuck out—were never worth it. We learned to let it go, and not ask questions, or we'd regret it.

At least not until my mother was on her deathbed.

Then she'd told me that not only had she known of my father's whereabouts this entire time, but that I had a *twin* sister.

My mom had moved as far away from Hostel, Texas as she could possibly get and had married another farmer up in Iowa. I'd grown up on a farm, just like my siblings had done with my biological father.

However, the problem with my step-father was that he hated my guts. He'd hated me with such a passion, in fact, that he'd shown it every single day of my life.

And without my mother there to be the buffer between us, I had nothing left holding me there.

So I'd taken a risk and moved to Hostel, Texas.

I'd bought my own land, although it was just a small amount—twenty acres—and made an attempt at meeting my family.

The moment my sister saw me, she'd thrown her arms around me like we were long lost twins—though, technically, we were. Apparently, my father hadn't kept my existence a secret like my mother had theirs.

From the moment we met, it was like the twenty-six years separating us had never happened.

And now, three and a half years later, we were making up for lost time.

The place I bought when I'd arrived was actually touching the land that I assumed belonged to Evander.

Though, if I had to guess, Evander actually owned quite a bit of it. There was property along the Old Highway with an old, run down house at the front of it. And surrounding it was a shit ton of trash, old abandoned furniture and more junk than I could name.

I felt like shit.

The people of this town had treated that property like a dump, and they didn't give a shit that they'd done it, either.

"He sure has filled that body out, though. Prison was good for him."

I felt sick at Edith's words.

Prison was good for him? What the actual fuck?

Prison wasn't good for anyone.

And then I berated myself.

I didn't know that man. All I knew was what I'd observed of him now, and that was very little. I'd met him at the feed store, sat with him at dinner, and he'd said all of twelve words. Also, he'd carried some of my bags to my truck.

That was it.

There was literally nothing else that I knew about the man to know whether he was a good man or not.

My instincts were always spot-on, though. I knew when a person was bad. I also knew when a person was good.

I'd had this ability since I was young.

It was just something about a man or woman that made me feel what kind of person they truly were, and Evander hadn't struck me as bad.

The women to my left, however, had all struck me as bitches from the moment that I'd met them with Trixie.

I'd hated them on sight, and I hadn't made any attempt to get to know them, even though I took my nephew to practice at least once a week.

The coach, however, he'd always struck me as being an inherently good man.

He was a mechanic at the one and only shop in town and had also been in the Marines for nearly a decade. Now, I'm not saying that all men that are in the military are good men, but the majority of them are. And Boone Trent was one of the good ones.

And now that I thought about it, he was also part of the Hail crew that everyone in town was always talking about—the same towing/auto recovery company where Evander's tow truck was from.

Small world.

"Where do you want me?"

Evander's voice brought not just mine, but every woman's head in a thirty-foot radius of him, up.

We all stared.

"Just go over by the dugout and toss them the weighted balls," came Boone's distracted reply. "I'm going to throw each kid a bucket of balls, and you can have the ones on deck. When I'm done, I'll call for the one you're working with. Okay?"

He grunted something in reply, and then started walking to the balls that were on the ground.

The red ones that were the size of normal balls, but they were squishy and weighted so that when they were hit, they didn't go very far.

He picked them all up in his hand.

All freakin' five of them.

Sweet baby Jesus.

I could pick up two. Two!

He picked up five!

Those hands had to be the size of dinner plates they were so big, but the one and only time I'd felt him touch me, it'd been a soft touch. One that had been just a brush against the skin of my arm.

Dear God.

I needed to get a grip.

But did I stop watching him? *Hell no,* and I wasn't the only one, either.

***

Two hours later, DJ, my nephew, and I were walking toward the truck.

He was in high spirits due to hitting a ball over the fence—a home run. I, on the other hand, was still torn in two.

My sister had cancer.

Jesus, this had to be a nightmare.

Maybe tomorrow when I woke up, it'd all be a dream.

However, I knew it wouldn't be. I wasn't that lucky.

"Thank you, Coach!"

I was startled to look up and see not the actual coach, Boone, but Evander standing beside me, handing DJ a ball.

"Went and picked it up after the last batter was up. Good hit."

Then he left, leaving me staring after him.

"Jesus, that man is big."

I looked over at Edith and offered her my best smile.

"Have a good night," I called out with false cheer.

Edith grimaced. "You, uhh, too."

Bitch.

The drive to Trixie's home was enough to nearly break me, and when I tried to come inside, she stopped me.

"I need to talk to my family, Kennedy," she whispered, looking away. "I haven't told the kids yet. We're going to tell them here in a minute once everyone's cleaned up for the night."

I leaned forward and wrapped my arms around her.

"Okay, Trix. Call me if you need me, okay?"

When I pulled away, her face was wiped of all expression.

"Yeah, I'll do that."

Then she closed the door carefully in my face and locked it for good measure.

A feeling of dread washed over me.

This wasn't right.

Something else was going on here, but without forcing my way in, I couldn't really do anything about the feeling without seriously pissing her off.

I knew my sister. I knew that she had a short temper and was quick to jump to conclusions.

I wouldn't force her to allow me to stay if she didn't want me to, but I would come back tomorrow.

And then, I'd force her to talk.

Lani Lynn Vale

CHAPTER 5

If you don't like chickens, you can stay outside.
-Welcome mat

Kennedy

Other than my sister being on my mind, there was one other person who was in my head and wouldn't go away.

If I wasn't worrying about my sister, I was worrying about him.

Why, I couldn't tell you.

I'd had all of four encounters with the man, but each time I did see him, even if from a distance, it was enough to send shock waves through my body.

I wasn't the only person that watched him, though.

Yesterday, when I'd been at the grocery store, Evander had been there, also.

He'd been two people ahead of me in line and everyone had stared. The checker that'd been ringing up his food. The security guard who was getting the money for the security place that deposited the money for them. The manager had his hand on his phone like he was ready and waiting for Evander to go off and start shooting people.

Then there were the women.

My God, even the elderly Mrs. Henry had stared.

Me, I stared probably more than most.

But he hadn't turned around. He'd kept his head forward, had paid in cash, and didn't look around as he made his way to his truck.

The only animation on his face at all had been when he'd opened his truck door and a German Shepherd had licked his face.

Now, I was standing less than ten feet away from him again at the feed store, and he was haggling with an old man about pricing for hay.

Hay which I needed, too.

Bad.

I'd been buying it from the feed store since my supplier had passed away, and I hadn't found any since that I could get without using a trailer—a trailer in which I didn't have.

I was also over spending nine dollars and fifty cents a bale, which was bad since I went through it as fast as I did.

I was listening unrepentantly to him talk with the old man and suddenly his eyes turned to me.

"Can I help you?" he asked.

There was no anger in his voice. In fact, there was nothing. No inflection. No, why are you staring like a weirdo. *Nothing.*

"Yes, actually. I need some hay, too. Can you get us both some, me one round roll like you're getting, and I'll pay you for the use of your trailer?"

He stared at me so long that I started to fidget.

Why had I done this? Could I leave without him seeing?

I glanced around and saw that I was in the middle of Tractor Supply, and the only thing around were the chicks that they kept in a large, six-foot cage to keep all the kids and people from reaching into the bins and petting the babies.

There was a very large metal yard art chicken that was standing about four feet away from me. Although it would've hidden my upper body significantly, the spindly legs wouldn't have done the job.

Needless to say, there was nothing for me to hide behind to shield my embarrassment.

When I finally looked back up to see if they were still looking, it was to find the old man staring at me like I'd grown a second head, and the big man, Evander, staring at the old man like I hadn't just interrupted his conversation.

I chose to run while I still had a chance.

Except, as I did, the box of chickens that I had in my hand started to go wild at the movement of my body.

I chose to keep going, knowing that at first, I'd be covered since the chicks in the bins behind me were making just as much noise as the ones in my hand.

When I'd come in here, it sure as hell hadn't been to buy more chickens.

In fact, I'd been adamant with myself. I would *not* get any more.

I had twenty-six at home and that was more than enough due to the size of the coop and the yard that I now had them in. If I got any more, I'd be pushing it.

I knew it. Yet, that hadn't stopped me.

It'd all started with me just going for a look.

Barred Rocks. Bantams. Rhode Island Reds. Copper Marans. Oh, and ducklings, too.

Then I saw the Blue Laced Red Wyandottes, and I became lost.

I'd seen a photo of the Blue Laced on Facebook a few months ago, and I'd fallen in love.

But when I'd gone onto the hatchery's website and seen that they don't ship the Blue Laced Red Wyandottes in anything less than an order of fifteen, I'd been able to corral myself.

Fifteen chickens, no matter how freakin' cute they were, weren't on the table for me at this point.

I was already pushing the limits of my twenty acres, and I didn't have the room to add any more pens to it without taking away from my giant ass's grazing pasture.

Jack Jack, my ass, was also the reason I needed a freakin' round bale of hay.

The bastard ate and ate. *And ate.*

He also decided that he no longer liked my goats and had started picking them off one-by-one when they came near his hind legs.

Which meant I had three goats in my backyard that chose to shit on my porch non-stop.

Then my UPS driver delivered my boxes directly in the shit.

Yeah, I needed more room. Yesterday.

And I needed six more chickens, Blue Laced Red Wynadottes or not, like I needed a hole in my heart.

Yet, there I was, darting down the aisles to hide from the man who looked at me like I was crazy.

So, I was staring at trailer hitches, when I didn't even have a trailer to hitch, wondering how long I would have to wait before the big man left, putting me out of my misery.

Jesus! What had I been thinking when I'd asked him if he could bring me a bale of hay?

Of course, he couldn't!

I was paying so much attention to my non-existent trailer hitch that I didn't even hear him coming.

And by the time that I *did* hear him coming, he was in the same damn aisle as me, barreling down on me.

But, by some miracle from above, an elderly woman stopped him, asking him what he thought of the trailer ball that she was holding in her hand, and whether he thought that it would fit her husband's boat or not.

When Evander made some rumbled reply, his eyes never leaving me, I realized that he was mad for some reason.

Why was he mad?

Was it due to me interrupting his conversation? Was it because he didn't want to bring me a bale of hay?

Whatever his reason, I decided that now was the time to leave and darted out of the end of the aisle, and all but ran to the front of the store.

However, when I got to the front it was to find not one, but eight other people in line, and I realized that I wouldn't be getting out of here any time soon.

I bit my lip as I weighed my options.

Stand in line, check out and hope that he didn't talk to me, or hide again. I was hoping that he'd leave before I found my way out of the aisles.

The question was answered moments later when I heard him say something, causing me to turn.

His eyes were once again on me, but I could tell that he was running out of patience.

When he rudely dismissed the person, this time a young woman who was in her twenties with breasts the size of cantaloupes, I realized that he really was set on talking to me.

I bit my lip, hunched down and started to hide behind the giant chicken, remembering what I noticed earlier about the legs, and took off again, right back to the trailer hitches by way of moving around the entire back of the store.

Past the dog food, the horse hoof trimmers and the generators.

When I arrived back at my original starting point, I took a look around and moved outside, thinking that would be perfect.

What I didn't think was that the door would be locked, causing me to smash not only my face, but the box I was carrying, into the glass.

"Shit!" I hissed, dropping down to the ground and immediately opening the box.

I'd meant to just take a peek, but the moment that the box opened, all fucking six of my new little chicks took that as their cue to jump out.

"No!" I squeaked, catching the first three very easily and placing them carefully back into the box.

The last few, however, proved to be devious little devils.

"Come here," I whispered, reaching behind one of the hitches for the cutest little chick I'd ever seen, only for it to dart away from my hand like I was the evilest thing on her little planet.

But I caught her when she thought she could fit through the end of one of the trailer hitches.

When she went to turn around and come back, she ran straight into my hand and I put her directly into the box.

When I came up to look for the other one, it was to find a pair of dusty, grime covered cowboy boots, within inches of my hands, firmly planted on the floor.

When I looked up, I knew what I'd find.

The man who was practically chasing me around Tractor Supply. Though, I had to admit, a lot of the reason he was doing that was because I was the one hiding.

But whatever.

I swallowed, went back on my knees, and looked at him.

He was holding my chickens.

And let me just tell you something.

A big, sexy man like Evander—holding tiny, fluffy baby chickens—was enough to cause every nerve ending in my body to start firing.

He had them cradled in his palm, his large fist curled protectively around the little terrors, and he was staring at me with a mixture of exasperation and humor tinting his features.

"You are incredibly annoying."

I winced.

"Here," he held the chicks out to me.

I took them and carefully placed it back into my box, then stood up with my spine stiff and straight.

"I don't know where you live, but I'll bring the bale by tomorrow around noon."

I nodded, finding it hard to swallow.

"Bye."

It wasn't until he was all the way across the store, which I could see because he was a head and shoulders taller than every single person he walked past, and out the door, that I realized that I hadn't told him where I lived.

I should've known, though, that he'd figure it out.

What I didn't want to admit, however, was that I was extremely embarrassed that he called me 'incredibly annoying.' I hoped he didn't find out where I lived, because then he would know that I was a whole lot closer than he realized.

And what would he do when he found out that he had an incredibly annoying neighbor, even if multiple acres separated us?

CHAPTER 6

Unless you're shooting a porno, I don't care about your live video.
-Evander's real-life words

Evander

I pulled my trailer over to the side of the road and pulled up Travis' number on the shitty disposable phone I got at the grocery store the day that I got out of prison.

Once I had him on the line, I wasted no time finding out what I needed to know, Kennedy Swallow's address.

Five minutes later, I was driving down the road, toward my own goddamn house, wondering how I would miss the new neighbor at the back of my property.

Though, I had to admit, I was a little on overload since I'd gotten out of prison.

I'd had a full-time job within twenty-four hours of getting out of prison, and pairing that with the way my property was used as the town's dumping ground while I was gone, I had plenty of shit to do.

I'd only made a tiny dent in the trash that'd been left, and I knew that it would take me several weeks more to get rid of it all.

I'd prided myself in keeping my property clean and corralled when I'd lived there, and the citizens of Hostel, Texas had shit on that while I'd been gone.

Lucky for me, and unlucky for some of them, I'd gone through some of the trash while I'd been cleaning up and found names and mail in some of the bags.

The dumbasses.

I'd even gone through an old broken-down dresser and found a man's diamond wedding ring—although it only fit me on my pinky—that'd been left in a drawer hidden in the back at the bottom of the dresser itself.

That was going to cost someone the money, but since it was left on my property as trash, I didn't care to return it like I might have before I'd gotten back to find my place being used as the town junkyard.

Passing my place, I turned down the side road that led down the north side of my land, and drove until I saw the first driveway that bumped up against the back side of my property.

And the moment I did, I started to laugh.

She had three goats that were on her back porch.

Two of them were standing on cardboard boxes watching me drive up, while the third was busy eating the bigger of the two boxes that the other goat was standing on.

I put the truck in park and had the door open in record time.

The moment my feet hit the cool earth, a quiet sheep dog stepped out from behind the porch steps, his eyes on me, very watchful of my every move.

I stopped, stared and wondered if he'd attack me if I came through the fence.

With only one way to find out, I shrugged and started forward.

The moment my hand hit the fence, though, he vaulted forward, barking.

Which then set off Gertie in the front seat of the truck.

Taking my hand off the fence, I raised it in the air in the universal 'I'm not going to come through your fence so you can eat my face off' sign and walked backwards a few steps and turned to my truck.

"Gertie, stop."

Gertie stopped, but he kept a wary, watchful eye on the enemy— the other dog who was staring at me like I was lunch.

"Mint, what are you going all crazy about..."

My breathing halted in my chest when I saw her.

She was staring at me, stopped beside the side of her house, with a shovel in one hand and what looked like a dead chicken in the other.

"Hey," she murmured. "What are you doing here?"

I pointed at the trailer that I was hauling with the two round bales of hay on the back.

"Brought you the hay." I refrained from saying, *like I told you I was going to do.*

She pursed her lips, went to lift her wrist that I could see her watch attached to, then grimaced.

"I have to bury my chicken," she said. "If you wouldn't mind giving me a few?"

I nodded, and she turned on her heel and walked away.

I followed closely behind her, stopping when I saw the amount of feathers everywhere.

"What happened?" I asked.

Her shoulders shook.

"A neighborhood dog came in and killed all my chickens."

My mouth went dry at the controlled anger in her voice.

"Did you catch it?"

She shook her head.

"No, but I knew the dog. He's been here before, but I've been able to catch him before he's done anything crazy." She looked at the mess around her. "I tried building a fence…"

She gestured to the pathetic looking fence that couldn't keep a house cat back let alone a dog, and then shrugged.

"I'm not so good at building things."

I could see that. Boy, could I see that.

I would not get involved here. *I would not.*

"Where would you like me to drop the hay?"

She pointed in the direction of the south field where I could see a lone donkey staring at the two of us.

"There," she gestured.

"Do you have a tractor?"

She shook her head.

I looked at all the property that she had, and my brows furrowed in confusion.

"How do you get anything done out here?" I asked.

She shrugged. "A push mower and a weed-eater for the grass." She started digging with her shovel, and I watched, confusion on my face, for the first two shovelfuls before I walked over.

Taking the shovel from her hand, I used half as much effort and did the same amount of work in less time, digging a hole about fifteen inches deep before looking at her expectantly.

"Good?"

She nodded, then picked up the bird that lay at her feet before depositing it inside. Gently. Reverently.

"Thank you," she whispered.

She held her hand out for the shovel, and I ignored it and scooped the dirt up myself, covering the bird.

"Thank you," she repeated, watching me work. "Thank you for bringing me the hay, too."

I nodded once.

"How many did you lose?"

She looked out over the yard.

"I don't know yet. All of them probably."

"All of them?"

She nodded. "Yeah."

"How many did you have?"

"Twenty-six."

Twenty-six. She'd lost twenty-six fucking chickens.

Holy shit.

"Where does the dog live?"

She gestured to the end of her driveway. "Straight across the way."

My stomach churned.

"I'm going to drop the trailer and go get the tractor. I'll get the hay and put it in there with the donkey."

She held up her hand, her dirt smudged face already set in an unforgiving line.

"Don't," she said. "You've done a lot already. I can get it."

"How?"

She stiffened. "What do you mean how?"

"How will you get it?"

She shrugged.

"You won't be able to lift it," I told her bluntly. "And I have a tractor. It's not a big deal."

She looked away.

Then her shoulders started to shake.

I bit my lip and wondered what I should do.

I knew that she was crying, but I didn't do well with criers.

I hated it, actually.

I hated the helpless feeling of watching someone else lose it. I hated not being able to do anything. I hated watching the tears fall down their faces, remnants of their pain.

"This sucks," she whispered, her voice breaking.

I looked down at my hands.

"Come on, you can come with me."

"Where?"

I took hold of her wrist, trying not to think about how freakin' small her wrist felt in my hand, and pulled her to the truck.

"You can come with me."

She followed behind me like a zombie, and I felt sick to my stomach at seeing her so dejected.

I didn't know this woman from the next, but she'd been kind to me when a lot of people in town hadn't. I felt some sort of kinship to her.

And I wouldn't leave her here, hurting, while she wondered how to fix something that was obviously not going to be an easy fix.

"Gertie doesn't know about personal space," I told her as I opened the door.

She got in, and I tried not to notice her backside, or how good her ass looked in her jeans as they stretched across said backside.

Ten minutes later, I gestured for her to climb up into the cab of the tractor. She did, and I climbed up directly behind her. Then promptly groaned.

I obviously hadn't thought this through.

Because, if I had, I would've realized that there was only one seat on the tractor, but I hadn't.

Now she was stuck either staying at my place, or riding with me on the tractor where there clearly wasn't room unless I wanted her in my lap.

But witnessing the fall of her face when she realized she'd have to stay behind was enough for me to reach down for her.

"Come on," I held out my hand. "You can sit on the fender, babe."

She sniffled. "My name is Kennedy."

I refrained from saying, 'I know' and patted her thigh. "Let's go."

We lived in a small town. It literally took less than two minutes to find out who she was. I didn't tell her that, though. She didn't seem ready to hear it.

***

I should've known that the person who would let her dog roam around free was the very same person who refused to give me my dog back just a few short weeks ago.

God, I hoped that she hadn't done that with Gertie.

Had Gertie been one of the dogs that had been terrorizing Kennedy's place?

I highly doubted it.

He wasn't the type to care about that type of thing. He was more of a laze around and be watchful, kind of dog.

The work he used to do with me and my unit in the military had been a bunch of hurry up and wait kind of shit. But when we were actually on missions, he had his work cut out for him.

But, during our time in the Middle East, we'd seen our fair share of chickens. Not fuckin' once had he even paid them any mind. Not. Once.

But this woman, with her other dogs that were roaming the neighborhood, didn't seem like such a great veterinarian. I mean, what kind of vet would just let her dogs stray around the area without caring what they did while they were out?

Apparently, this kind of vet.

"Ma'am," I said, nodding my head. I knew this wasn't going to go well, but I decided to let her have a chance at fixing this the easy way. "Your neighbor witnessed that dog," I pointed to the one that was laying on the ground, his paws stained with blood, "running away with her chicken. He dropped the chicken while he was running back here to your place, but she's got twenty-six dead chickens right now. That was her way of earning income."

The vet's mouth pursed.

"My dog hasn't left the yard."

Liar.

"Your neighbor begs to differ," I said. "She witnessed that one running away."

The woman slammed the door on me, and I growled.

My eyes turned to the dog in question, and I sighed.

It didn't look like a mean dog, but that didn't make it any less destructive.

Taking the steps two at a time, I walked back down to the truck and stopped just as a police officer pulled in.

He parked directly behind my truck, and got out, his eyes never leaving me.

The moment that I saw the man, I wanted to punch him.

I didn't, though.

"What are you doing here, Van?"

I crossed my arms over my chest.

"I'm here because I got news that my neighbor's chickens were killed and this woman's dog did it."

The officer looked at the dog in question and his brows furrowed.

"Which neighbor?"

"Kennedy Swallow." I gestured across the street. "She lost twenty-six chickens today all due to this little shit head's dog being out."

The officer sighed. "You can't harass the neighbors, Van."

I headed to my truck.

"I didn't harass them," I told him as I opened the truck door. "I came by to inform her of what had transpired. Harassing means that I continued to bother her, which I didn't. I told her, and she slammed the door in my face. Then you arrived. Simple as that."

I got into my truck, started it up and was unsurprised by the officer arriving at my window.

The look of anger he gave me wasn't surprising. What was, was the way he slammed his hand on my window.

"What the fuck, Van?"

I lowered the window and stared.

"What the fuck, what?" I sneered. "Officer Asshole."

My brother's hand reached through the open window and fisted in my shirt.

I didn't flinch. I didn't do a goddamn thing but stare at him.

"What are you going to do?" I asked. "Hit me?"

"I did everything I could, you know."

I laughed humorlessly.

"Yeah, I can tell." I flexed my hands out in front of me. "That's why I have a phobia of dropping the soap now, right?"

He gritted his teeth.

"Let me go or hit me. Either way, fuck you."

My brother's hand unclenched from my shirt.

"I did everything I could," he repeated.

I shrugged.

If that was 'everything' he could do, then he was a fuckin' joke. Now I remembered why I didn't have much of anything to do with the bastard. At least my sister didn't try to pussy foot around the fact that she didn't care.

"Wasn't good enough, now was it?"

With that, I rolled up my window and was thankful when my brother yanked his hand out of the way.

He watched me for a few long seconds, before growling and walking away.

I stared straight ahead, my eyes periodically going to the rear view.

And the moment he was out of my way, I backed out, not sparing him another glance.

My brother could go to hell.

He hadn't helped me when I needed him, and he sure as hell hadn't helped matters by allowing my place to get utterly trashed.

Needless to say, there wasn't a damn thing my brother could do to make this all right, no matter how hard he tried.

Lani Lynn Vale

CHAPTER 7

I've been watching so much porn lately that I spit on my hot dog
before I put it in my bun during lunch.
-Things not to tell your parents

Kennedy

The call to the market in town where I sold my eggs was enough to rip my heart out.

"I'm sorry, Ms. Swallow," the owner of the mercantile, Kevin Yates, apologized. "I can't hold the spot for you, but when you get back up and running, I'll definitely consider buying from you again. It's been a pleasure. I'm sorry, but I just don't have a choice."

I just don't have a choice.

Those words played over and over in my brain, and I wondered what I should do.

I'd never set out to allow my chickens to become my full-time business, but it'd turned out that way.

I'd been making upwards of a hundred dollars a week from them, and now, I didn't have any income at all.

Luckily, I had money in the bank and I could, technically, start over. I had a nest egg thanks to my mother's life insurance policy, but I didn't want to touch that unless I had to.

And when I did get up and running again, there was still no guarantee that I'd have a chance to sell eggs to the same supplier again.

Not to mention it took at least five months before a chick was old enough to start laying eggs. And even then, it'd be several weeks more before they were laying them consistently enough to give me eggs every day.

I was lost.

So lost, in fact, that I was practically staring into the eyes of the big man that was somehow on my property before I even realized he was there.

"Ummm," I said, startled. "Hello."

He grunted something at me.

"What?"

"I'm here to help you build a fence."

I looked at my watch.

"It's seven in the morning…on a Saturday."

He shrugged. "Used to be up at six on the dot. Been that way for four years now. Can't just turn it off because I want to."

I didn't know what to say to that.

"Okay," I said. "But I don't need a fence anymore."

I looked around at my empty yard.

I'd gotten up this morning out of pure habit, slipped on my yellow rain boots with the flying chickens all over them and had gotten all the way out into the yard before I realized there was literally nothing for me to do anymore.

Normally, I would've walked out, opened the coop door, and then fed and watered my chickens.

However, since none of them were alive any longer, I didn't have to do that.

My other Saturday morning ritual was to go into town, buy some feed and then grab a donut.

Now, there wasn't a reason for feed.

I had my six baby chicks, sure, but they didn't eat anywhere near as much as my older ones had.

I took a step from one foot to the other, and then happened to look down at what I was wearing, and nearly groaned.

Shit!

I brought my eyes up almost painfully, and looked at him, despite the embarrassment that was running through my veins.

"There is a reason," he said, drawing my attention away from my 'Mother Clucker' tank top, and my hot pink shorty shorts that were clearly way too small for me, yet I continued to wear because I liked them and they were comfortable. I would be changing this outfit as soon as I got a chance.

"There's a reason for what?" I wondered.

What was he talking about?

"To build the fence. You got more chicks the other day…didn't you?"

I nodded.

I didn't want to think about chickens anymore.

They were depressing.

"Well, I know a lady that's looking to get rid of her entire flock. She's moving into an apartment, and they don't let them have them at her complex."

I blinked.

"Why is she moving?"

Why was that my question? Surely, I could've come up with a more appropriate answer, like 'Hell yes! I love chickens!'

But I didn't.

Thank God.

My mouth could run away from me every once in a while.

Well, if I were being honest, I would admit that it was more than 'every once in a while' and more like 'all the fucking time.' But who was I to give a number to something? I wasn't God!

"She—the woman that used to own the corner property up there—is moving into a retirement home. She's got about ninety chickens…"

"Whoa!"

He grinned. "Don't worry. Most of them are meat birds. She's going to be processing those before she goes, but she has twenty-three egg chickens—if that's even what they're called—and was going to process them, too, but I told her you might be interested in them."

My heart started to pound.

"That's the sweetest thing I think I've ever heard."

He shrugged. "They're not your birds, but it's something. And she said she has about eight dozen eggs she has nothing to do with if you're interested in those, too."

My eyes were filling with tears.

"Can't get them if you don't have a fence, though," he grumbled, his eyes going down the driveway where it snaked through the trees. "I visited the neighbor whose dog you said attacked your chickens. She wasn't willing to pen it up."

I looked away, suddenly overrun with the need to throw myself in this man's arms and hug the shit out of him.

I was able to refrain, though.

Barely.

"That doesn't surprise me," I said softly. "Her father was a vet, and used to be a whole lot more neighborly than her. I used to trade him a dozen eggs once a week for antibiotics for my chickens every six months or so. When I suggested that to her, she laughed in my face."

His mouth—that beautiful freakin' mouth—curled in annoyance. "I got one better than that."

My brows rose. "You do?"

He grunted something in reply and walked to his truck. "You mind if I let Gertie out?"

I shook my head in the negative. "No, that's perfectly fine."

He opened the truck door and the large German Shepherd I'd seen a few days ago hopped out.

He was limping slightly, and I crouched down.

"He's beautiful."

And that was when I saw that Gertie only had three legs.

How had I not seen that when I'd been sitting next to him in the truck on the way back to his place? Was my head that far in the clouds?

"He's something," Evander agreed. "You ever seen him before?"

Confusion swept over me. "You mean other than when I was with you the other day?"

He nodded.

"No."

His eyes softened.

"The woman vet has been taking care of him since the old vet died. Seeing as she lives right across the street, I was hoping that he wasn't one of the ones that came over here and terrorized your chickens."

I shook my head immediately. "No, he wasn't one of them. Only hers, which started showing up about a month after Doc Civil died. This yard's been hell ever since."

He nodded.

"You know I was in jail?"

I froze, wondering if I should tell him that I knew everything there was to know about the man.

Even though I didn't gossip myself, that didn't mean that others in the area didn't talk about him.

Hell, I sat two hours a night on Tuesdays and Thursdays listening to the other mothers discussing the man's best and worst features.

I knew that he'd slept with four of the moms on my nephew's team, and every last one of them was willing to go for more if the man gave them the time of day.

I knew that he was in jail. I knew that his family hadn't taken care of his place while he was gone. I knew that his brother was a police officer and that he'd been the arresting officer in Evander's case. I knew that Evander liked pineapple and mushrooms on his pizza. I knew that he was a size fourteen shoe and that he was six-foot-six-and-a-half and wore a size thirty-six by forty-two in pants. I also knew that he went on a jog every single day and that jog took him past my house, down the road all the way to the high school and through the main part of town and back.

I knew everything about him that one could know…except his secret, inner thoughts.

"Yes," I finally admitted.

He didn't seem to act surprised by this knowledge.

In fact, he was pretty relaxed…he seemed almost relieved that I wasn't hearing it for the first time from him.

Which, I guess, was a good thing.

In my eyes, it meant that I was purposefully spending time with him despite knowing that he'd been to jail.

Which, I still wanted to know the full story.

I'd heard the gossip of the why, but gossip and the truth were sometimes two very different things.

I wanted to hear the story straight out of the horse's mouth.

"I had the vet, the old one that used to be there before the woman, watch over Gertie."

I nodded.

"We signed a contract. I paid him every cent of his money for the four years that he'd be watching Gertie and then I went to jail."

I started to get an inkling of what he was about to say.

"And she wouldn't give Gertie back?" I guessed.

He shrugged.

"Gertie and me share a bond that nobody, not even you with your dog, would understand."

"Why not?" I accused.

I looked over at my dog, my livestock protector who I'd had to lock up in the yard because the vet's dog kept attacking him anytime he was out, and sighed.

"Gertie and I were in Iraq and then Afghanistan together for over four tours," he said. "We went through some crazy shit and came out standing on the other side … Well, mostly. He was retired after he was caught in a roadside bomb and lost his leg. We were separated for six months while he healed, and then while I got out. But the moment we reunited in the states, it was as if not even a day had passed."

I smiled at his story.

"That's the most I've ever heard you speak," I told him bluntly.

He shrugged.

"She tried to keep Gertie on account of the fact that I'd been gone for four years and hadn't taken care of him while she had."

"How did you get her to give him to you?"

He grinned.

"Gert managed that on his own," he explained, patting the dog that was at his side on the head. "Kicked up a fuss, and the attendants let him out because they thought something was wrong in the lobby. There wasn't anything wrong, he just heard me."

I was amazed. "I'm not trying to hurt your feelings here, but how the hell did he even remember you?"

Evander grinned. "Told you. We have a bond that transcends time and shit. I could've been gone for the rest of his life, coming back when he was on his deathbed, and he'd still remember me."

I couldn't stop the smile from forming on my face.

"That's great news," I whispered, excited to see his face so animated.

That smile, however, died.

"All in all, that bitch ain't gonna do anything about her dog. What I would suggest for now is the fence. What I would suggest for later is thinking about suing the bitch for damages and loss of income."

My eyes widened.

"I can do that?" I asked in surprise.

He nodded. "You sure the fuck can."

CHAPTER 8

At first I cared, but then I was like, 'Nah, fuck you.'
-Text from Kennedy to Evander

Kennedy

"We need nails."

We needed nails? Okay.

I didn't even ask, I just got into his truck with him.

Though, I likely would have stayed if he hadn't held the passenger side door of his truck open expectantly.

So there I was, in the middle of Lowe's, walking behind him as he made his way, swiftly and efficiently, to the hardware department where the specific kind of nails he needed were kept.

I'd been in Lowe's a hundred million times, at least, and I still didn't know my way around.

Maybe it was a male thing to instinctively know where he's going.

That, or maybe he'd just bought nails and knew where to find them.

Whatever the reason for his powers of nail location, I wasn't complaining.

What I did complain about, however, was the fact that he wanted to pay.

"No," I said sternly, stamping my foot. "No, no, no, no, no."

He ignored me and handed the lady thirty dollars in cash.

"Phone number?"

He shook his head.

"Don't got one."

The checker raised her brows. "You don't have one?"

He shook his head.

"You can have mine," I said, rattling off the digits. "Thank you."

She smiled at me, her eyes going up to the man at my side, and then shook her head.

Her eyes, I could tell, were full of fear.

And she wasn't so sure what to think about the man at my side.

He was big, yes.

He was dark, yes.

He had a beard, yes.

He had tattoos, yes.

He was scowling, yes.

Okay, he was scary.

But not *that* scary.

Not the way she was staring at him, anyway.

He grunted something when she handed him the receipt, and then her eyes went wide when he grabbed my elbow and pulled me along.

I went with him, not complaining in the least that he was touching me.

In fact, I quite like that he was touching me. Nobody ever touched me. Not my sister or my father.

I'd had one boyfriend in all of my life, and that one only lasted all of twenty seconds because he couldn't handle my life.

Then again, not many people could handle my life.

When I was fifteen, my older sister got cancer. When I was sixteen, she died. When I was seventeen, my mom got cancer. She battled it for the last few horrible years of her life before she died, too.

I spent years dealing with cancer, and I still hadn't recovered, not even years later.

Now, I was dealing with it again. Although Trixie had made it clear that she didn't want, nor need, my help at this point.

She wanted to spend as much time with her family as she could, and that didn't include me. Honestly, that hurt.

It hurt bad.

The only thing she was willing to allow me to do was to take my nephew to baseball practice twice a week.

And when I brought him home, Darren met me at the door.

It was obvious that he didn't want me to come in, so I hadn't.

My life sucked.

It really did.

Except, the big guy at my side was making it better, even if he wasn't very cheery while doing it.

We'd just exited the store when he stopped and stared at something in front of him.

"What is it?" I asked.

He gestured to something in front of him.

It was a truck. A big one that looked like it was lifted up so high that I'd have to take a running leap to get into it.

It had a light bar across the top, and I swear to God that it looked like the truck had a unibrow.

Then I noticed all the lights.

"Whose truck is that?" I asked, taking in the multiple bars that resembled red and blue emergency lights on the bumpers.

"According to my paperwork," he pulled out his phone and pulled up a screen in an app that I didn't recognize. "It's Officer Dale Rogers' truck. He's behind not one, not four, but six car payments."

I blinked.

"You're kidding."

He shook his head.

"And that means…" I left it hanging, wondering if he'd answer me.

"That means we're picking it up and taking it in," he grinned.

He grinned.

Grinned…with teeth showing!

I'd never seen him smile before, but if that grin was anything to go by, it was life changing.

And man, did he have pretty teeth. The smile changed his face, transformed it from mean and scary to sexy and dark.

If there'd ever been a time where I wanted a man, it was now.

I wanted him, and I wanted him bad.

And the scary thing was that I thought he might know it.

"Gotta go get my truck," he murmured.

I nodded.

"You think you can go in there and distract him while I do my thing?"

I froze in place.

"Yeah…" I hesitated. "But I don't know what he looks like."

Evander turned his phone around and showed me the screen.

There was a bunch of writing on the screen. Then, in the top right corner next to his name and address was his picture.

He was a male, in his late twenties, with a cruel looking smile. He was dressed in his dress blues from Hostel Police Department, and I knew the instant I saw him exactly who he was.

"I'm not sure he's going to believe that I want to talk to him," I finally said.

His eyes came down to me.

"Why not?" he asked, sounding confused.

His eyes roamed my body, starting at the top of my head, and moving down to the tips of my toes, and what he saw was obviously something he liked if the small grin he gave me was anything to go by.

But it was there and gone so fast that I almost wasn't sure that what I saw was real.

"Because, just last week, I turned him down for a date…" I hesitated. "And the week before that, I turned him down, also. I'd never willingly go up to him."

He looked down at me, studied me for a few long seconds, and then nodded.

"Then let's hope like hell that he doesn't come out while we're doing this."

Then he walked to his truck, and I assumed, expected me to follow.

I did, hurrying behind him to keep up with his long legs, and then came to a stop when he went to the passenger side and held the door open for me.

"T-thank you," I murmured, walking towards him.

With the way the cars were parked on either side of us, the fit between him and the door was a tight one, making me squeeze so close by him that I felt his body heat all along the length of my back.

I shivered as I reached for the bar to help pull myself in, and gritted my teeth as I started to hop up on one foot while also trying to keep myself from falling on my face.

"You need a step on this thing," I muttered.

It wasn't big, per se, but it was compared to my lack of height, and the truck's taller stature.

I'd just resigned myself to jumping when I felt a tug on my pants, and then felt my ass being lifted by the belt loop of my jeans.

I went with it, not stopping to think until I was sitting on my bottom.

That was when I realized that the man that I found super sexy had his hand near my ass, and I nearly squealed.

"Thank you," I murmured, managing to keep it at an octave that was conducive with hearing.

He slammed the door shut without a word, and I decided that the momentous occasion of his finger in my belt loop was nothing to him while it was everything to me.

Jesus, I needed to get a hold of myself.

To keep my eyes from being on him when he got in, I reached for my seatbelt and looked toward where the truck was parked.

"Do you think you can get the truck that quick?" I asked him, eyeing the cars all around it.

He started to laugh, and I turned at the sound.

I liked how his throat worked. I liked how he stared at me with his eyes shining. I liked him.

A lot.

"Yeah, honey," he snorted. "I think I can get it quick."

And then I watched as he pulled out of his parking spot, rolled up the rows of cars, and then expertly backed up to the big, jacked up truck in under a minute.

Then, I continued to watch as he got out, hooked the truck up, and was back inside in less than two.

"You've done this before?" I asked him breathily.

My heart was pounding!

Why could I not breathe, you ask?

Because the man was hot as hell.

Watching him in the truck's big ass mirrors while his muscles bunched and released was enough to send my libido into overdrive.

The light sheen of sweat on his skin, though? That was enough to send me to my knees.

"Do you think he'll noti…" I stopped when I saw a man running outside, his loaded down cart full of wood and concrete trailing behind him.

"Yeah," Evander said. "I think he'll notice."

I snorted a laugh, then settled back into my seat as he drove us out of the parking lot without a care in the world.

CHAPTER 9

*Basically, if you can pull off a beard, you can pull off my
underwear.*
-Fact of Life

Kennedy

"Cock sucker," I grumbled, bending down to pick up the nail.

I heard a snort, but when I looked at the man at my side, he looked no different than he usually did. Stoic and blank.

I went back to the nail I'd just picked back up off the ground, placed the U-shaped piece of shit back across the wire that was strung tight across the four-by-four post we'd sunk into the ground, and bit my lip.

Very carefully, I aimed the hammer in my hand against the nail head. Once I thought it was in well enough, I pulled back and hit it a little harder, only for it to go flying again.

"Goddamn you, you little piece of shit," I growled.

That's when the big man at the other end of the fence—the same man who'd started directly next to me going the opposite way as me—started to laugh.

"How do you do this?" I groaned. "I don't understand!"

He shook his head. "One of the nail ends is a little longer than the other. Get that side in a little first, and then give it a good whack."

I glared at the offending nail that was winking in the sunlight from its position deep in the grass and grumbled something unintelligible. "Whatever."

Bending down, I picked it up again, and then adjusted my bra where I was storing the other nails—the ones I hadn't had use for yet since I hadn't even gotten a single one of the fuckers in.

"Like this," he said, suddenly beside me.

I blinked at his abrupt nearness, but dutifully watched him do the nailing, putting in four in the blink of an eye.

"Maybe I'll just be your nail holder," I offered, staring at his muscular forearms.

He started to chuckle. "I guess that's okay. I need another one."

So we worked in companionable silence, him pounding nails and me pulling them out of my shirt and handing them to him.

We did that for a while, then we stretched more fence.

Fence I hadn't been aware needed to be stretched when I'd done this myself.

Then again, I'd just used chicken wire and staples which, apparently, wasn't how it was supposed to be done. *Surprise, surprise.*

It was while we worked on one of the last posts that it happened. The one single thing that changed my life.

"Here, hold this," he said, handing me the piece of the fence. "Pull up while I nail it."

I did as asked, trying not to press my breasts against him as I did.

My forearms were shaking with the abuse I was putting them through, and I was fairly sure that I was the picture of sweaty, unattractive female.

Yet, I kept going, because this man was doing me a favor, and no matter how bad my forearms hurt and my hands screamed, I was going to work until I could no longer stay on my feet.

"Do you have a nail?"

I looked at my hands that were holding my fence up, and then down to his knee that was holding it down below, and then shook my head. "Not in my hand."

His eyes went down to my shirt where it was bulging unnaturally with nails and then bit his lip.

"Just do it," I gasped. "My arms are about to give out."

He reached forward and took the first nail that was on top, barely even touching any of my skin.

It was just a brush—a barely-there, brief little graze—of his thumb against the inside of my left breast. But it was the best touch I'd ever felt in my life.

I would remember it for the rest of my years.

I'd also remember the look in his eyes at the moment his fingers skimmed across my flesh.

I chose to be a good girl, though, and instead of letting out the involuntary moan creeping up my throat, I buried it.

Turning away from his eyes which stayed glued to mine, I bit my lip and stared straight ahead.

It took him another couple of moments to do his thing, and by the time he was done nailing in all five nails, I was on fire.

Not literally, but my arms were screaming, and I was fairly sure I'd need a new pair of panties.

Being this near to him was hell on my nerves.

He was literally setting me on fire and he hadn't even done anything but run the pad of one thumb against the side of one of my boobs.

An innocent touch, yet it was enough to tell me two things.

One, I was a hoochie. Anything would be better than nothing.

And two, I was falling for this big, silent man who had done nothing but talk to me for a few short minutes each time I'd seen him.

But, as they say, actions spoke louder than words.

He'd helped carry heavy bags to my truck. He'd buried my chickens. He'd built me a freakin' fence.

So, no, I didn't think that this big man was as bad as everyone in town was making him out to be. I knew for a fact that he was kind, caring and a whole lot of awesome.

I just had to prove that to him.

Oh, and figure out how the hell to make him fall madly in love with me, because I was well on my way to going down hard for him.

***

Four hours later, I was sweaty, tired and on the verge of tears.

"Are you sure you don't want to stay?" I asked hopefully.

"Can't," he answered. "Gotta take the truck to the lot and drop off my load."

I nodded, wiping my hand off on my pants.

Then, I held it out to him.

"Thank you for your help," I whispered. "I really appreciate it."

He looked at my hand for so long that I wasn't sure that he was going to take it.

But he did, and when he did, his hand engulfed my much smaller one.

"You're welcome," he muttered. "You made me a grand today by allowing me to help with your fence."

"What?" I asked, startled.

He gestured to the driveway where his truck still had the one he'd picked up earlier hitched up in the air with the towing rig. "A grand on that one."

I blinked, then turned to survey the truck.

"I think I'm in the wrong business."

He grunted. "This business isn't for women. No offense," I snorted at his words. "But you'd be eaten alive."

I shrugged, not knowing what he meant, but deciding that I'd get him to tell me all about his job.

"You want to have lunch tomorrow?" I asked.

He shook his head. "Got to work tomorrow."

"Dinner?"

He stared at me, watched my eyes, and then seemed to come to a decision.

"Look…," he growled. "I've been to jail. Being seen with me is like signing your own death warrant in this town. If you like delivering your eggs to the Mercantile and making money, you'll forget you even know me in public."

Then he was gone, leaving me with my heart somewhere around my knees.

But I made a promise to myself.

The next time I saw him, I would go out of my way to let everyone in the entire town know exactly what I thought about the man.

CHAPTER 10

It only takes one slow walking person in the grocery store to
destroy the illusion that I'm a nice person.
-Fact of Life

Kennedy

Low and behold, that moment came the next day.

I was in town, picking up new nesting boxes for my chickens that I
was going to go pick up tomorrow, when I saw the familiar tow
truck out in front of the diner. The diner that nearly everyone in
town ate at during lunch.

Making a split-second decision, I turned into the parking lot and
came to a stop directly on the back side of the tow truck that I only
assumed was Evander's.

My thoughts were confirmed moments later as I made my way
inside the diner.

He was sitting at the back of the diner, his back to the room.

Somehow, I knew he was acutely aware of everyone and
everything that was happening in the diner.

I knew the moment he knew I was there because he stiffened.

He didn't bother to look up from his tea, though.

He stayed exactly where he was, hunched over a book that was
down on the table in front of him.

Without asking if it was all right, I parked myself in the seat directly across from him, and stared.

"Hello," I smiled at him, causing him to bring his head up.

He blinked.

"What are you eating for lunch?"

He looked at his empty plate.

"Had a tuna melt."

I nodded, and then flagged down the waitress, who was doing everything she could not to appear like she was staring at me.

"Can I have what he had, but a water instead of a tea?"

The woman, Phyllis, blinked. "Sure, darlin'."

She stared at me, and then glanced at the man at my side, then shook her head.

"What are you doing?"

I returned my gaze to the man in front of me.

"What you expected me not to do. You were expecting me to ignore you, correct?"

He nodded.

"Well then, yes, I'm not ignoring you. And I'm actually kind of peeved that you think that I would."

"Peeved?"

I nodded. "Peeved."

"What, exactly, is peeved?"

"Pissed off. Annoyed. Irritated," I informed him.

His lips twitched.

"Wouldn't want to make you pissed off."

I narrowed my eyes at his sarcastic tone.

"What are you, a buck ten?" he asked. "What could you do if you were pissed off at me?"

I opened my mouth to tell him exactly what I could do, but the server interrupted us.

"Your water," Phyllis set it down, then immediately left.

I snickered.

"They really don't like you," I told him.

He shrugged.

"They think they have a good reason."

They think. Not they do.

"I'm meeting the lady for my chickens later," I told him. "Do you want to come?"

He stared at me. He did it for so long that I was on the verge of asking him what was wrong, but he smiled.

The smile made my heart stop.

My whole fucking life went from gray and bleak to so fucking sunny that I had to take a breath at the beauty.

When Evander smiled… Jesus Christ, it was poetic.

He was gorgeous normally, but when he brought that smile out…it literally melted my heart.

"Are you asking me, in front of witnesses, if I want to go out on a date with you?"

I opened my mouth to deny it, then closed it.

"Yes," I said finally. "Come be a crazy chicken man with me."

He snorted, then leaned back in his seat.

"I don't get off until four."

Those words made me so happy.

It wasn't a no!

Over the next hour of the lunch rush, I ate while Evander spoke. At first, it was about nothing consequential…then he started to tell me about himself.

Whatever barrier that had been erected between Evander and I had been destroyed.

And now he actually *spoke* to me.

"My doctor said I should start killing people."

I blinked at him, wondering what he was going on about.

"What?" I asked, setting my half-empty glass carefully on the table.

He nodded. "At least, that's what I got out of it."

"What was said, exactly?"

He was funny. Really funny.

He had a sense of humor that made me want to laugh out loud—which I would have done had we not been in a busy diner with nearly half the occupants already watching us with their speculative eyes.

"Well, he said I should reduce the stress in my life."

"And that turns into killing people in your mind?"

He nodded. "The only stress I have is this shithole town and the people in it. Since I can't get rid of the town, I'm thinking the people need to go."

With that, I burst out laughing.

"You're fucking nuts." I shoved a piece of my sandwich into my mouth.

I liked this man.

He had a wonderful sense of humor, and it was sad that the people of this town didn't see what kind of treasure they had in the man.

"Did you really go to the doctor?" I asked, the thought just now occurring to me.

He shrugged.

I sat up, my eyes narrowing.

"Evander."

He sighed. "I was having chest pains."

I gasped and nearly toppled the table over.

"Chest pains!" I cried out. "You're only thirty-four!"

His mouth tipped up at the corner.

"Actually, it was because the chain on the winch snapped and popped me straight in the chest," he supplied. "I had to get checked out per company policy. That, and Travis was there when I was recovering the vehicle and pretty much forced me to go."

My eyes were still wide.

"You had a chain…what?" I asked a little too loudly. "Let me see!"

His eyebrows rose.

"You want me to take my shirt off in the middle of a diner where everyone and their brother is currently watching our every move?"

"Fuck everyone else," I practically snarled. "Let me see."

Let me tell you something about Evander.

He didn't have a bone in his body that was modest. I'd learned that the hard way.

Or the nice way, depending on how you looked at it.

I'd been working that fence with him for the last two days, and he'd gotten all sweaty. Sweaty enough, in fact, that he'd deigned it too hot to wear a shirt, and he'd taken it off.

He didn't see anything wrong with the act…and I didn't think it was something I needed to tell him that men didn't do when they were in front of a lady…a lady who they barely knew.

Since today had been the first day that he was back at work, after his two days off, I hadn't seen him yet today.

Because if I had, I would've noticed early on that he wasn't moving right. And sitting down, I hadn't quite been able to put the dots together.

Evander had this grace about him, despite his height and bulk.

He looked like a great big cat that was always on the hunt for something—what, I didn't know. What he didn't do was favor one side and move stiffly.

Something in which I'd noticed, yes, but since he'd been sitting with me for over an hour now, I'd chalked it up to being stiff from remaining immobile for that long.

He was so private and asking anything about him that he didn't freely offer up, I'd realized, was very hard for him to answer.

It was as if he had to think everything he said through, and if I asked him a question that he hadn't thought about having to answer, it was like pulling teeth.

He didn't like it.

So I'd learned to be quiet and let him steer the conversation where he wanted.

Or at least I tried to.

Sometimes I wasn't always so successful.

He started to pull up his shirt, keeping the left side that faced the diner down with one hand, and raised it until I could see the dark, purpling bruises on his chest.

There was a distinct purpled chain link mark on four spots across his chest. One right below his right nipple. One about an inch above it to the right. One directly in the center of his breast bone, and one more just below his collarbone.

"Ohhh," I winced. "That looks terrible."

He shrugged, then pulled his shirt down.

Too soon.

I hadn't gotten my fill yet.

Dammit.

"When does your sister start treatment?"

I looked up to find his eyes on me, and I started fidgeting.

"Tomorrow," I hesitated. "I think."

"You think?"

I nodded. "Yes, the last I heard it was tomorrow. I haven't heard anything to the contrary yet, but as of a week ago, at the doctor's office, it's then. They put the port in two days ago...that, however, she never asked me to go with her to. They, my brother-in-law and sister, just did it without telling me she was having the procedure done, and before I could get up there once I did know, she was already on her way home from the hospital."

He stared at me for a few long seconds, his brows furrowed. "That sounds kind of shady."

I shrugged. "They kind of pushed me out of their life once they found out that she has cancer. It's almost as if…"

I couldn't finish the sentence.

Saying it aloud almost made it true, and I didn't want to think the worst of my sister.

"As if what?"

I should've known the big man sitting across from me wouldn't let my evasion pass.

I cleared my throat.

"Almost as if they're blaming me for what's happening to her," I said. "They haven't outright said it yet, but I can read between the lines. The only time we have together is when I'm getting my nephew to take him to practice."

"I've noticed that they hadn't made one yet."

Ever since that first time I'd seen Evander at practice, he'd shown up at nearly every one of them.

The only one he missed was the one two nights ago when I'd left him at my house finishing my fence.

"Why do you allow them to use you?"

"She's not using me," I immediately argued. "She's just doing the best she can."

He made an sound that clearly let it be known that he didn't agree, but I chose to ignore it.

"I'm helping her because I love her."

That shut him up.

"Don't know about love. But I know about loyalty, and they wouldn't show the same thoughtfulness if it were you in the same position."

I didn't have anything to say to that.

He was right.

Nobody. Not my brother, who barely even gave me the time of day, my father, who only called me because he needed something, or my sister, would ever offer me help if I needed it.

My sister, I could forgive.

My father, I could forgive.

My brother, I could also forgive.

Which was the problem.

I was a freakin' pushover, and I couldn't stop it.

"I've been asking around about you."

My brows shot up.

"You have?"

He nodded.

"What did they have to say?"

His eyes felt like they were boring into my skin.

"Honestly?" he asked. "Not fuckin' much. They, the boys at the office, had no clue who you were. And since I'm not liked by the rest of the town, I didn't learn much of anything but what I overheard some of the people say at the farmer's market today."

"You go to the farmer's market?" I asked in surprise.

I loved the farmer's market!

He grinned. "Yeah, the shit grown locally is ten times better than the stuff you can get at the store…plus, there's someone there that I wanted to see."

"Who?"

His grin widened. "A guy named Don. He's the honey guy that sits on the corner of the road right outside of town. He waves at everyone."

I clapped my hands together. "I do know him! I buy honey from him every so often. I even bought a walking stick once."

He winked.

"I bought a walking stick there once, too." he explained. "Then, on the way home, my bike broke down. When I got off, I placed my helmet on the ground behind the back tire. When I was going back to the bike, I semi tripped on the walking stick and sort of stumbled. To keep myself from falling, I moved down into the ditch further than I intended."

"Yeah?" I sat forward.

"And a car hit my bike going almost seventy miles an hour."

My mouth dropped open.

"You're saying that this walking stick tripped you, and you moved out of the way in time to avoid getting ran over?"

He nodded.

"Holy shit."

He nodded again.

"From then on, every time I see that man, I stop to talk to him. He's become one of my best friends."

I smiled, my lips spreading so wide that my face nearly hurt.

"I can only buy so much honey," I told him. "But I do like him. I'll have to make a point to stop by there more, though."

His grin was sweet.

"He's a lonely old man, and I've missed him these last four years. I think he'd like that." Then he sighed. "I have to go back to work, pretty girl. Otherwise, I won't get to go all chicken mad with you."

I grinned. "I think I can deal with that."

He winked, then stood up.

Before I could say another word, he left, stopping only at Phyllis' side so he could hand her a fifty.

Then he was gone and I was left staring after him with my heart on my sleeve.

CHAPTER 11

It's too hot in Texas for titties.
-Kennedy's secret thoughts

Kennedy

I felt like shit.

Complete and utter shit.

Today was the day of Trixie's first chemo treatment, and I didn't even know how the hell I was getting to the hospital.

My truck wouldn't start, and my father's car was in the shop for routine maintenance.

Stupidly, I'd taken it in yesterday for him and had started to walk home.

I was only about halfway home when I was discovered by Evander, who'd been on his way to my house to go with me to get the chickens.

He'd then yelled at me for not calling him.

When I'd explained, rather meekly, that I didn't have his number, he'd given me his card and told me to program in his numbers.

I had kept the card in my hand for half the night, looking at it, wondering if I should or not.

If I had that number…if I used it…then I wouldn't stop using it.

He would have me calling him at all hours of the day, and I would send him memes. I wouldn't be able to help myself.

But now I had to.

I looked down at the card for the fourth time.

I shouldn't call him.

But he'd said *anything*.

A ride wouldn't be too much to ask, and since we didn't have taxis where we lived, he was sure to understand, right?

I started dialing the numbers.

It rang twice.

"Van."

"Uhh," I hesitated. "This is Kennedy."

Everything about his abrupt demeanor changed. "Hey, pretty girl. What's wrong?"

The worry in his voice filled me with hope.

Hope that he may someday feel the same way about me that I knew I felt about him.

"My truck won't start, and my sister's treatment is today."

"I can be there in thirty minutes. Is that enough time?"

I looked at my watch.

If I had a thirty-minute drive to the hospital, and thirty minutes to wait, that was an hour. I had to be there in an hour and fifteen minutes. That would be plenty of time, right?

"Yes, that's perfect," I said, even though it was cutting it kind of close.

But they'd deal.

I really thought that Trixie likely didn't want me there anyway.

But I'd be there and wait for her to finish and, hopefully, show her that I would support her no matter what.

"Okay, I'll be there in a few."

Evander arrived in twenty-two minutes, and he was sweaty as hell when he got out and walked around to the passenger side of the truck and opened it.

I smiled at him, then smiled wider when I saw Gertie in the front seat.

"Hey, boys," I smiled, or tried to anyway. "Y'all look kind of dirty."

That was an understatement.

Evander was filthy. He was covered in grease and what looked like mud—but not red mud. Gray.

The dog wasn't in much better condition.

"We were in the middle of a fuckin' mud pit trying to get a monster truck unstuck. It took three tow trucks to do it."

I blinked. "I took you away from a job?"

He shrugged. "You wouldn't call me unless it was important. And Travis already had it mostly under control. It wasn't a big deal."

I decided not to argue, but I did get in the truck and question him about it the moment his ass touched the opposite seat.

"Why were you in the middle of a mud pit?" I asked.

His grin was wicked.

"The guy put his monster truck—and when I say monster truck, I literally mean a monster truck—up for collateral on the bond for his brother. It was a five hundred-thousand-dollar bail and the only thing he had in equity was his truck that he used for shows. When his brother didn't show for court, he knew the truck was going to be taken…so, in a fit of anger, he took it to the middle of the biggest mud pit he could find and parked it. He didn't think we could get it."

He sounded like he was having a grand old time, and the smile on his face was enough to put me in a remotely better mood.

"That's exciting," I said softly.

He nodded. "One of the more fun ones, for sure. Where do I need to go?"

The mood lost, I told him how to get to the hospital, and then waved him off as he pulled into the car port of the hospital entrance. "Don't get out, honey. I'll just go in here, and I'll catch a ride home."

His eyes were hard when he disagreed. "No, you'll call me when you need a ride, and I'll come. I just need about thirty minutes to get here."

I tightened my lips together, and then nodded once. "I guess I can do that."

He touched one finger to my face through the open truck window, and then winked. "Go or you'll be late."

I went and managed to look over my shoulder only three times before I had to turn the corner.

The last look he gave me, as I went, was enough to stick with me for the next four hours while I waited for my sister, who never showed.

***

"Hello?"

I finally got my brother in law to answer his phone, and when he did, he sounded angry and upset.

"Darren!" I cried. "I've been trying to reach you and Trixie for the last four hours. Why isn't she at her appointment?"

He grunted something.

"There was an accident, and Trixie is in the hospital."

My brows furrowed.

"What kind of accident?"

"She was on the tractor mowing last night, and it tipped over on her."

I practically ran across the street as I made my way to the second tower of the hospital—the part where the emergency room and the patient rooms were.

The moment I arrived on the floor that Trixie was on, I found Darren in the waiting room, waiting for me.

I was so confused.

So, so confused.

"What do you mean the tractor tipped over on her?" I asked in bewilderment. "Why was she on the tractor in the first place?"

Darren glared at me.

My stomach was cramped so hard that I couldn't breathe.

"I don't know," he lied.

Lied.

I knew when the man was lying.

Trixie had told me he had a tell, one I thought was actually kind of cute...until now.

He scratched his chin, and his nose twitched.

Not that I couldn't tell just by the tone of his voice.

Trixie hadn't been on that tractor willingly.

Trixie had told me she hated being on the tractor and only got on it if Darren needed her help with something.

It scared her, and she literally couldn't stand being on it for more than a few seconds, which most of the time was all that Darren needed from her.

This time, he'd said that she'd been mowing.

Mowing my ass.

"So how is she?" I asked hopefully. "Can I see her?"

He shook his head. "This is the ICU. She's not good, Kennedy."

My heart started to hammer.

"What did the doctor say?"

I could tell he didn't want to talk to me.

Not at all.

But I needed to hear the diagnosis. I needed to know if I would lose her, too.

"She has crush injuries," he said through tight lips. "She's in renal failure. She has fluid on her brain that they're pretty sure will need to be alleviated right now, and her blood pressure is through the roof… They're not sure any of that will matter at this point because her cancer has made her body very weak."

I sat down, no longer able to feel my legs.

"When can I see her?"

She was going to die.

I knew that like I knew that tomorrow the sun would rise.

"Visiting hours at the hospital are eight AM to twelve PM, and two PM to six PM. I'm bringing the kids later. Normally, they don't allow kids, but since she's not expected to make it through the night, they're waiving the rules for now. Tomorrow morning will be the best time for you to see her."

I couldn't take those kids' last chance at seeing their mother alive away from them. Tomorrow would have to be okay.

I closed my eyes.

"Okay," I whispered. "You should go, though. There's a baseball practice tonight that I know DJ won't want to miss…if you don't mind me walking with him."

He nodded.

"Thanks," he muttered. "Have a good day, Kennedy."

Have a good day.

Have a good day?

How could I have a good day when my sister was dying?

I knew she was, too.

I also knew that this wasn't an accident.

What I didn't know was if this was Darren's idea or Trixie's.

I stood up and started walking, not sure if I wanted to call Evander or not for the ride, but in the end, I knew that he was the only one that I could call at this point.

I pulled out my phone, put it to my ear, and waited.

"Evander?" I asked the moment that he picked up.

"You ready?"

"Yeah," I nearly choked. "I'm ready."

"I'll see you in fifteen. I'm close."

He hung up, and I sat down next to the exit of the hospital and cried.

CHAPTER 12

I feel like there's something missing in my life, and I can't figure out what. A person? A puppy? A burrito?
-Text from Kennedy to Evander

Evander

"You're crushing on the girl?"

I would've hung up on my boss had he been on the phone.

Since he wasn't on the phone, but on the radio, I could do nothing but turn the radio off. But to turn off the radio meant that I wouldn't hear the rest of the boys talk about me, and that wasn't gonna happen.

I couldn't let them get the wrong idea about Kennedy and me.

So, to change the subject, I countered Travis' question to me and shot one right back at him.

"So…I hear that you knocked a woman up."

There was complete silence on the airwaves—not a single one of them said a word.

Not Pack. Not Gallagher. Not Anderson.

And sure as fuck not Travis.

It was likely that even more were listening in on the conversation, but the four main players that were previously speaking were no longer full of taunts.

Now, it was the boss in the hot seat, and they weren't willing to say a word, that or they just knew something that I didn't.

Either was a possibility.

"Over a beer, my friend, I'll share that story with you."

I snorted, lifted the mic up to my mouth, and said what needed to be said.

"You mean you let *that woman's* demons become your own, and you chose to let your head rule where your heart should…am I correct?"

Travis didn't say anything.

"Anyway, I'm picking Kennedy up from the hospital now, I gotta go."

Travis was stupid.

He'd always let his past control his future, and obviously, a pregnant woman who he deeply cared about was one of those things that he denied himself.

Which, in turn, was why he was stupid.

He'd had a bad thing happen to him once. He'd done nothing wrong.

Yet, Allegra Levaux—the person in his past whom he couldn't seem to get away from—ruined any relationship that he tried to have.

I'd just decided that maybe an intervention was in order when I pulled into the parking lot and saw Kennedy.

She wasn't alone.

The arresting officer with my case, my brother, was hovering over her as she sat against the building, staring at her with concern.

I pulled the truck under the portico and threw it into park before storming over to where Kennedy was on the ground with her back leaning against the black glass of the hospital's entrance. Her arms were around her upraised knees, and her face was buried in them.

Her brown hair was up just like it was this morning, but now it was askew, hanging off to the side of her head where it covered her left ear.

The only thing I could see was her right ear, and that was stained pink.

Her shoulders were shaking, and I could tell that she was crying— mostly by the sobs that I could hear ripping painfully from her chest.

"Kennedy!" I called out the moment I could see her. "Honey, what's wrong?"

I pushed my brother aside and dropped down to my knees beside her.

The moment she'd heard my voice, though, she'd lifted her head.

When I was in front of her, she threw herself at me and buried her face into my neck.

Tonight … tonight, I'd tell her that she shouldn't hug me in public. Tonight, I'd tell her that I couldn't be what she needed me to be.

But for now, now I'd hold her. Now I'd give her the comfort that she needed. Now, I'd be what she needed me to be.

"Honey, what's wrong?"

She sniffled loudly and then moaned.

"My sister was in an accident, and she's in the ICU," she said through her tears.

My brows furrowed.

"How'd that happen?" I asked her.

I wasn't aware that having chemo was dangerous enough to put someone into the hospital, and I said as much.

"S-she never made it to the hospital. Apparently, last night, she had an accident on the tractor, and it tipped over on top of her. They d-don't expect her to l-live," she hiccupped.

My eyes closed as I heard the pain in her voice.

Oh, God. That was terrible.

Not to mention incredibly unlucky. First, cancer. Then she falls and gets crushed by her tractor? She had to be the unluckiest woman in the world.

I didn't say those words aloud, though. She didn't need to hear my inner thoughts, which were morbid at times.

"It wasn't an accident," she whispered into my ear.

At first, I wasn't quite sure what she was speaking about, but then understanding dawned.

"Shit."

I looked up at my brother who was still standing there being nosy.

"Go away."

My brother narrowed his eyes.

"As soon as I make sure she's okay."

I grunted something at him, then turned back to Kennedy.

"Pretty girl," I lifted my hand and smoothed it down the length of her ponytail.

It was soft. So freakin' soft. I wanted to do nothing more than run my fingers through it for hours.

But I couldn't.

I couldn't give her the wrong impression. Couldn't allow her to get to that point with me.

I knew she had feelings. I knew that she cared about me.

But people who cared about me always left. Mostly because they were forced to.

It started with my mom. She'd been the one true constant in my life…then she'd died. My sister? She'd been my best friend. But then I'd introduced her to some boys from my graduating class, and she'd started to get into drugs. Which my brother had then resented me for. He'd been my other best friend, but me leading my sister down the path of evil, despite me not intending to do it, had driven a wedge between us.

My sister had kicked the drugs, but I knew that she resented me as well seeing as she'd been indifferent to me ever since.

My brother, at least, tried to act like he cared…well, that is until he arrested me four years ago and watched while I was put into prison for something I didn't do.

But having this crying woman in my arms was enough to make my entire heart feel like it was exploding from the inside out.

I wanted her.

I wanted her in my arms.

I wanted her under my skin.

I wanted her in my life.

Which meant that she wasn't the only one having feelings. Feelings that I couldn't afford to have for her.

Not if I wanted to make sure she was safe.

The people in this town had a hard on for me, and I wouldn't subject her to that.

No way, no how.

"Let me take you home."

She clung to me tighter when I went to pull away, and my heart felt so fuckin' heavy that my breathing was choppy.

"Come on," I urged, standing up.

When she still didn't let go, I pulled her up into my arms and then walked around the driver's side of the truck, ignoring the way my brother continued to watch since he suddenly turned into the nosiest person on the planet.

I got the door open, and I climbed up into the truck with Kennedy still in my arms, slamming the door once we were inside.

"I need you to sit in the seat so I can drive, honey."

She nodded against my chest but still didn't move.

So I did the only thing I could do, I put the truck into drive, moved out of the spot I was in and ignored my brother's glare that clearly said he didn't approve of what I was doing.

Whether it was driving with her still in my arms or having her in my arms in the first place, I didn't know.

And to be honest, I just didn't care.

Not one single fucking bit.

Once parked in the back of the lot, away from prying, unapproving eyes, I held her while she cried.

Her body was so small against mine.

It felt like she was a tiny thing.

Which, I guessed, she was.

She was much smaller than my sister's five-foot-five height.

I'd say she was probably around five-foot-two, and weighed considerably less than the weight I bench pressed on a daily basis.

My arms practically wrapped around her twice, and goddammit, did she smell good.

Like fucking fruit…apples and something else I couldn't quite place.

What hurt the most, though, was the way the sobs wracked her tiny frame. The way she shook in my arms, and felt like she would break at any second.

"You're killing me. You're killing me, and I don't think I care," I whispered into her hair.

Peaches. The other smell was peaches. It was coming from her hair, though, and not her skin.

She sniffled and pressed her nose even deeper.

"My sister's going to die."

I closed my eyes as her pain washed over me.

God, I didn't know what to do or say to make her feel better.

At this point, though, I wasn't sure there was anything I *could* do.

I wasn't God. I couldn't bring her sister back and magically heal her. I also couldn't take away the pain.

I literally could do nothing, and I felt helpless.

Something that I told her.

"Just take me home," she whispered.

I squeezed her tighter.

"Are you sure you want to go home?"

She nodded against my chest.

"Yes," she exhaled shakily. "Darren said visiting hours are almost over, and tonight he wants to have just the kids there to say goodbye."

I couldn't argue with that.

But I also knew, from experience, that if the patient was terminally ill or dealing with life-threatening injuries, that they would waive the regular rules of the ICU if the patient's prognosis was grim and it was likely that they would lose their battle imminently.

"I'm sorry, Kennedy."

I practically heard her swallow.

"I'm so tired."

I smoothed my hand down the back of her head, then back up again, coming to a rest just underneath her ponytail.

Her hair felt like silk in my hand.

"Scooch over, Kennedy."

She squeezed her hands tight, almost as if she wasn't going to let go, and then did.

That was when she realized the position we were in, and blushed.

Though, that might've been a trick of the light against her face that was already blotchy due to all the crying.

Whatever the reason, I ignored it and flipped the console up for her to move over a little easier.

"I have to stop by my place and get Gertie," I said. "I dropped him off at home during lunch so I could come back for you, and he wouldn't have to sit in the hot truck."

She nodded her head.

"Okay."

Then she crawled off my lap, very carefully I might add, giving me an unencumbered view of her ass with those tight jeans stretched across it as she moved to the passenger's seat.

The moment she was in her seat, I looked away before she caught me and put the truck into drive.

"Do you want something to eat?"

Her sniffle broke my heart. "No, thank you."

I drove in silence to my place, looking over at her periodically to make sure that she was okay.

Each time I did, she would turn her face up to me, giving me her eyes, and I felt some sort of pull that was practically begging me to touch her in some way.

I managed to hold back the urge to pull her hand into mine, but only just barely.

By the time we pulled into my driveway, I was a fucking mess of pent up aggression.

Before I got out, though, she halted my movement.

"Evander?" she whispered.

I looked at her. "Yeah?"

"I don't want to go home."

I looked at her, really looked at her, and gave her what she wanted.

"Your chickens fed? The dog?"

She nodded. "Fed everything before I left. They should be good until at least tomorrow morning."

I got out of the truck and walked around to her side, opening the door for her.

She slid out, then stared at my yard.

"You know," she said, looking at all the junk. "This really pisses me off. I had no clue that all this junk wasn't yours. Otherwise I would've done something about this."

I laughed humorlessly. "Nothing you could've done. The town's set on not liking me. Hell, they barely tolerate the rest of 'Hail Raisers,' either."

She started up the front walk, having to swerve off of it to miss a huge anvil that someone had dumped right in the middle of my walkway, and kept walking.

I pulled my keys out of my pocket and then stepped to the side as I opened the door to allow Gertie to come out.

He walked straight to his usual spot and did his business before following us right back inside.

Kennedy watched this all with a small smile on her face, and then walked into the room.

"This is beautiful," she whispered the moment she stepped inside.

I looked at it from her point of view.

"Amazing, really," she continued. "The chandelier doesn't really seem like your style, though."

I grinned. "I like old stuff. When I was building this house, I went to a few antique stores and old barn sales to make sure that I got authentic stuff. The wood from the house came from the old barn that used to reside right at the top of my driveway. That's this," I said referring to the wall.

She touched the wall where the faded red paint from over a hundred years of painting came from, and hummed.

"I watch a lot of HGTV. Jo and Chip would've gone bonkers over this."

I snorted.

"They might have, yes."

I touched the saw marks from the blade that was used to cut the piece of cedar, then showed her. "This is some of the best wood that you'll ever find," I told her. "Do you see this?" I indicated the marks, and she nodded. "Saw blade marks. And this," I pointed to a knot. "I fucking love little details like this."

She wandered around the room, and I headed to the bedroom. "Make yourself at home. I'm going to go shower and change."

She made some noncommittal sound, and I walked down the hall that led to my bedroom, then started stripping. My boots were the first thing to get kicked off, followed by the jeans, my underwear, and finally my shirt.

The moment I walked into my bathroom, I flipped on the faucets for the shower…and nothing.

Not a single drip of water.

I narrowed my eyes.

Then a stray thought occurred to me.

I'd seen the water meter guy today when I'd been repossessing his car.

He wouldn't…would he?

I growled and walked to the wall where my towel hung, then slung it around my hips as I stalked out of my bedroom and down the hallway.

"Hey, does the water work in the sink?" I called out, stopping in the middle of the living room.

I heard something clink—the faucets being turned—and then a muttered, "No."

I walked back to my room and bent over, fishing my phone out of my pocket.

The moment I had it in my hand, I searched through my contacts for the water company, and pressed 'Go.'

The phone rang twice before a harried sounding woman answered it.

"Hostel Water Company," she sang.

"My water's off," I said to her. "I want to know why."

"What's your name?" I heard her shuffling some papers on her desk.

I rattled off my name and address and waited for the clicking to start, but it never did.

"I'm sorry but since it's so close to five, I won't be able to do anything about your water being off until the day after tomorrow."

I narrowed my eyes, then lifted my wrist to glance at my watch.

"It's four thirty. I have plenty of time until five."

She murmured something, and then held her hand over the phone, before saying something more.

It took a minute for her to get back on the line, and when she did she said, "Can I have your name again?"

I gave her my name, then waited some more for her to type my information into the computer.

"I'm showing here that there was a late payment," she lied.

Lied through her fuckin' teeth.

"I can pull up a copy of my receipt," I said coolly. "But I came up there and paid to get the water turned on. Paid a deposit, and then prepaid a few months, too. Trust me when I say that my payment wasn't late. I can even tell you who I spoke to."

Frustration and anger were clear in my tone, and that was apparently leaching through the phone line.

She didn't reply for long moments. "I'm showing that your check bounced."

I growled. "Lady, I didn't pay in check form. I paid cash."

Some other muttering, and then shuffling of more papers before, "Oh, I see. Well, then I'm not sure why your water was switched off but, unfortunately, all technicians are out on other service calls. They can't…"

"Let me tell you something," I said. "If you don't come up here right now and turn it back on, I'll come down there and file a complaint on your ass, as well as that little fucker's ass who thought he'd perform his own personal act of justice by turning my water off after I repossessed his car because he was late on his payments. And if I have to go that far, I might as well go ahead and file harassment charges against y'all as well."

There was a long pause on her end before she said, "I'll see if I can get someone out there before six pm."

I grunted at her. "You do that."

I hung up my phone and tossed it angrily on the bed before turning around, only to stop when I saw Kennedy there, staring.

"They turned off your water?"

I grunted. "Yeah, you hear the rest?"

She nodded.

"That happen often?" she asked.

I shrugged. "People are assholes and retaliate. Most of the time, it's not that big of a deal. The cars I repossess are sometimes for banks, sometimes for bail bondsmen who didn't get their money back because the guy didn't show for his court hearing. I even helped the local bondsman repossess a house before I went to jail."

She hummed. "That seems like a pain in the ass. Why would you ever put your house up as collateral?"

I shook my head. "This case was more complex than that. Apparently, a man bailed his sister out who'd been forging checks. But what he didn't know was that she'd been doing it for so long that he probably shouldn't have bothered bailing her out. Chick was headed straight to jail, and the brother didn't even know it. So he bails her out, puts his house up as collateral, and the moment she's out, she runs. Doesn't show up for the court appearance. Doesn't even say thanks to the brother. Just up and leaves and never comes back."

She moaned. "That's so terrible."

I agreed.

"Do you feel bad when you do this?"

The question, though innocent, was like a sour spot in my stomach.

"I don't enjoy doing anything of that nature," I offered. "But someone has to do it, and it pays good. I don't enjoy being the bad guy."

She nodded. "Do you want to take a shower at my place?"

I was about to reply with an affirmative when someone knocked on the door.

I walked that way, not stopping until I had the door open wide.

"What?" I asked.

"I just had a call from the woman at the water company saying that you were harassing her."

I growled. "They turned my water off. You can say that is harassment, but it's not. I called to see why, since I paid this month and next month's payments, not to mention a fucking whack of a deposit, in cash mind you. So no, I wasn't harassing her. I was trying to figure out why the fuck my water is off when I'm paid up."

He stared at me, I guessed to gauge my seriousness in the matter, and then went for the mic on his shoulder.

"Call the water company back and tell them that they have less than thirty minutes to get the water to this place back on, or this'll become a police matter," Walter said into the mic.

The dispatcher at the other end said something to affirm that she would and then he stared at me almost as if he were waiting for something more.

Something more that I wasn't willing to give him.

I knew what he wanted to ask. Was I okay? Would I ever forgive him? Would he be okay with what had transpired while I was gone?

But some movement at my back had him glancing behind me, and then he muttered something short and abrasive before saying his goodbyes.

"Who was that?" Kennedy asked as my brother made his way down the driveway.

I turned to find her standing there, surrounded by my shit, in my fuckin' house, and felt my belly get tight at the pleasure of having her there.

"My brother," I said. "He's hoping I'll forgive him."

Her brows furrowed. "What did he do that he needs to be forgiven for?"

I shrugged, but resigned myself to telling her the whole truth.

"My brother was the arresting officer on the charges that were thrown at me," I said. "And while I was in prison, he shacked up with my ex-girlfriend and got married. Then divorced her within a year."

Her mouth fell open.

"Your brother did that?" She pursed her lips. "He doesn't look like you."

I grunted. "Different moms."

"Oh," she looked down and her eyes widened.

I couldn't help the way my cock was getting hard. Having her in my house was doing things to me that I hadn't felt for another woman in a very long time.

She ignored it, though, so I did, too.

"It wasn't that he got together with my ex. It was that he did it within a month of me being put in jail that pissed me off. He didn't even wait for the grass to grow back where I used to park my truck in her yard before he made his move."

She winced.

"That's terrible," she admitted. "I don't even know what to say."

I shrugged. "I don't either."

Then I walked to my bedroom. "To answer your question, yes, I'd love to take a shower at your place."

And that's what I did.

Two hours later, we were back at my place, and she was sitting on my couch with a glass of wine in one hand and a slice of pizza in the other.

"I just don't know why she would've been on the tractor..."

She continued to talk, and I continued to listen, but what she was saying sounded just as suspicious to me as it did to her with the way she was describing it.

"I don't know what to tell you," I said. "To be honest…maybe she did it knowing that she was going to hurt herself. Maybe she didn't want to face cancer. Maybe it genuinely was an accident. Maybe he had a part in it. I don't think we'll ever know unless you can get your sister to tell you and that doesn't sound like something she can do at this point."

She moaned and took a bite of her pizza, tearing it viciously with her teeth.

"Fuck."

She looked up at that muttered curse that blasted from my lips and raised her brows at me in silent question.

"Nothing," I muttered, shifting on the kitchen chair. "You want another piece?"

She picked up the last piece that was in the box and set it carefully on her plate, eyeing my hands as if I'd grab it from her.

"I'm not going to take it from you," I muttered to her. "Done with the ranch?"

She nodded, taking another bite of her pizza.

I stood and gathered up my trash, as well as the pizza box and ranch, before putting it all where it belonged—the pizza box on the back porch, the trash in the trashcan, and the ranch in the fridge.

By the time I was done, she was already working on her last bite, but she was watching me as I moved around the kitchen.

"What?" I asked, leaning against the counter and crossing my legs to hide my discomfort down below.

Her mouth turned up slightly on the edge, and I saw that she had something green between her teeth.

"You have something in between your teeth," I told her. "Right here."

I gestured to the spot with my finger, and she reached forward and removed it before saying, "Well, since you were so nice, I think I might need to tell you that you have a ton of food in your beard."

I grinned. "How long has it been there?"

I didn't bother to lift my hand to remove it. I had Cinna Stix from Dominos that I was about to devour. It would be counterproductive to wipe my face clean at this juncture when I was about to stuff it full again.

"You're not going to get it even after I told you?" she asked with incredulity.

I shrugged. "Why bother?"

Then I showed her why when I reached for the box of Cinna Stix, ripped open the plastic covering on the icing, and then dunked the stick into the icing, coating it three quarters of the way up with the ooey, gooey goodness.

"You have a bottomless pit for a stomach," she pointed out as she started to lick her fingers clean.

I eyed her.

"I was in jail for four years. I was told what to eat. When to eat. How much I was allowed to eat. And that only had to do with eating. Don't even get me started on the sleeping shit."

Before she could reply, though, the windows started to rattle with the sound of an oncoming storm.

"Oh, no," she said. "I hate storms."

My brows furrowed.

"Why?"

She shrugged. "Scary, I guess."

She was lying, but there was no reason for me to press the issue. That would only solidify the 'I care' feeling she was likely already getting from me, and I didn't need that.

She didn't need it either.

Lani Lynn Vale

CHAPTER 13

I speak three languages. English, profanity, and bullshit.
-Evander to an unsatisfied customer

Evander

After I finished my food, not stopping until every last piece of cinnamon was cleaned off of my plate, I gestured toward the door.

"Are you ready to go?"

She was shifting from foot-to-foot, I'm sure wondering what exactly I would want her to do now that she was finished eating and that she had calmed down.

At my words, she stiffened and then nodded.

"Yeah, I'm ready." She stared at me for a few long seconds, then started heading toward the door. "I need to check on the animals, anyway. With storms, they sometimes get confused and do stuff they wouldn't normally do."

"Like what?"

"Drown themselves," she muttered.

I stopped when she said that. "What do you mean?"

"Well, chickens aren't the smartest animals in the barn," she pointed out. "For instance, if a chicken was watching his other chicken friends get attacked, he'll just stand there and watch once he gets himself a safe distance away. Me, I'd run the fuck away and not stop until my legs either fell off or gave out. My chickens? Every last feather was found in the main yard, meaning that not one of them ran any further away than their usual hunting grounds."

I understood what she meant.

"They're a little slow, I'll give you that," I amended.

She smiled up at me and walked out the door when I opened it for her, not stopping until she was beside my truck waiting for me to deal with the unlocked door.

I locked it, then headed toward her side of the truck.

Once there, I opened it, but stopped when I bumped her with the door due to the closeness of my body to her back.

She chuckled, and I cursed silently as her backside made contact with my still hard-as-a-rock shaft.

She didn't shrink away from it, though, so maybe it went undetected.

It didn't.

When I finally stepped back and allowed her entrance to the truck, her face was tinged with pink, and she was no longer meeting my eyes.

Wonderful.

The sky overhead rumbled again with thunder, and I offered her my hand to help her along.

She took it gratefully and hefted herself into the seat, then pulled her feet in tight to allow me to close the door.

I tried not to find the blush on her cheeks fascinating, but once I was back in the driver's side, I realized that that was futile.

I couldn't keep my eyes off the woman, even when I tried.

She was magnetic, and I wanted nothing more than to have her stay at my place and force her to hang out with me the rest of the night.

I was a lonely man! Surely, I deserved the company of a woman.

But then my brother's shock at seeing me with Kennedy earlier in the evening played through my mind, and I wondered if I could get away with threatening everyone's life that questioned why I was with her.

And I was again reminded that I wasn't good for her.

She was a good girl. She had a lot on her plate, and she didn't need my shit piled onto it.

We drove in silence back to her place, and by the time I pulled into the driveway of her house, I decided that I would walk her to the front door and then leave.

I should've known it wouldn't work out like that.

By the time I'd gotten out, opened her door, and then led her up to her front stoop, the bottom dropped out of the sky and rain started to pour down.

Though, that wasn't the problem.

What *was* the problem, was the way something ungodly loud crashed from somewhere inside her house.

"What was that?" I asked.

She ignored me and my question, then threw open her front door just to come to a stop when she saw the way her roof sagged by the front door.

"Oh, no," she moaned. "Shit, shit, shit!"

She snatched up some papers off the table directly under where a board had obviously broken through the roof due to something—

maybe extra weight from the rain on the roof—whatever the reason, it wasn't going to be fixed tonight.

And it likely would need a professional.

"Damn," I murmured, checking out the damage.

She mumbled something under her breath, and I turned my head down to study her.

"What?"

She sighed. "Karma."

"Why Karma?" I questioned.

She pursed her lips in disgust.

"That cop whose truck you repossessed?" she murmured, her eyes flicking to mine and away. "He asked me if I wanted help with my roof a few weeks back when I went for some new shingles. I told him no, that I would be able to handle it. Obviously, I was wrong."

I looked back up at the damage, and just then noticed the rotting wood that was exposed due to the ceiling collapsing. Then winced.

"I'll get this checked out tomorrow," I told her. "Anything we can do tonight will be just reserved for in here. The roof ain't happening in the rain, and the damage is already done."

I tried to close the door, and growled when it wouldn't close due to the shift of the house around it.

"And it looks like I'm staying here for the night," I said. "You got a couch?"

I looked at where a couch would normally be, and she made an aggravated sound.

"My sister needed one and couldn't afford one, so I gave her mine," she murmured, looking at where a couch might sit. "Dammit."

Then her eyes started to fill with tears, and I knew that I couldn't leave her.

And likely never would've been able to.

Not tonight…and likely not for a while after that.

She was under my skin.

I didn't know who I was kidding. It sure as fuck wasn't myself.

The moment the first tear hit the skin underneath her eye, I had her in my arms. When the second tear fell, it was against my chest. The material of my t-shirt soaked it up, then another, and another.

All I could do was hold her as a fresh wave of tears took her over, and I felt, once again, helpless.

I wasn't used to feeling helpless.

When I felt helpless, I tended to use my fists.

But, at this point, I wasn't sure I could use my fists again.

I couldn't take it out on Kennedy's brother-in-law, and I sure as fuck couldn't take it out on the dying sister.

I did the absolute only thing I could, which was gather her in my arms and pull her into my chest as I carried her down the hall to what I assumed was her room.

I wasn't wrong.

When I arrived at her bedroom door, I didn't bother to flip on the lights. Instead, I kicked off my boots and headed to the bed, holding her close the entire way down to the softest mattress I'd ever slept on.

We stayed like that for what felt like forever.

Then she fell asleep and still I stayed.

***

I laid in her bed for most of the night, her tucked up to my side, and listened to her breathe.

I should've left hours ago.

In fact, I would've left hours ago…had she not been wrapped around me like a second skin.

She'd slept for over four hours before she slowly woke, and even then, I stayed where I was.

The storm continued to rage around us, and I winced every time something sounded like it was creaking in the living room.

When I felt her bring a piece of her hair up to her hand and twirl it against my t-shirt covered chest, I couldn't hold it in anymore.

I had to talk to her.

"I have a military friend," I said to the ceiling. "He calls this weather baby making weather."

"It was one of his favorite sayings. 'It's baby making weather.' Every time it stormed. It couldn't be just regular rain, though. It had to be thunder and lightning."

"That's kind of funny," she giggled, and her hand started moving down the length of my chest, stopping just above my belly button before it moved back up again.

"I should go."

The abrupt declaration had her tightening her arms on me, holding me there as if that would actually stop me from leaving if I'd really wanted to go.

But since I didn't want to go, I allowed her to stay my muscles, and continued to stare at the ceiling.

"I'm a bad bet, Kennedy."

She snorted. "Everyone's a bad bet."

"You're not a bad bet," I countered.

She laughed humorlessly, her entire body shaking against my side. "Everyone in my family has had cancer at some point in their life. I'm the only one left standing that hasn't been affected."

She had a point.

"But you don't know that you won't ever get it. You're just assuming."

She shrugged. "Doesn't matter. Who wants to date a woman that has a seventy percent chance of getting cancer and dying before the age of fifty?"

I didn't know the answer to that question.

"You find that right person, and it won't matter to them," I told her bluntly.

Like it didn't matter to me.

If I'd been a different person...a better person...I'd take hold of her hand and never let go.

But I wasn't a better person. I was a criminal. Though I didn't commit the crimes I'd been sent to jail for, I'd done a lot of bad shit in my life. Killed a lot of people—sanctioned by the US government, sure. But still.

I had blood on my hands and that wasn't going to change.

"We don't have to actually make the babies," she told me, startling the shit out of me with her words. "Just practice. I don't want forever with you, Evander. Forever means a whole lot of shit, and I don't want to leave my family. My kids. My husband. Because I may not have cancer yet, but it's inevitable. It's gonna happen. And I just want someone to be with me in the meantime. When you're ready for it to end, we'll end it."

I was making a mistake.

A huge, hulking, I'm about to make the worst decision of my life—and maybe hers, too—mistake.

But I didn't stop myself from rolling over and pinning her beneath me.

I didn't stop myself from slamming my mouth onto hers.

I didn't stop myself from fitting my hips between her legs, and grinding my hard cock against her mound.

No. I didn't do anything to stop what I knew was about to happen.

Why? Because I was weak.

So *fucking* weak.

She pulled away from me and her lips started to skim along my bearded jaw, but I hadn't had enough of her mouth yet. Not nearly enough.

"Kiss me," I growled, pulling her hair and bringing her lips back to mine.

"I want to taste the rest of you, though," she said between breaths.

"I know," I muttered. "And there's plenty of time for that…*later*."

She kissed me back, her hands taking up the work that her mouth was doing earlier, smoothing them up and down the length of my spine, up my sides, down my chest.

Her legs wrapped around my hips, holding me to her tight, as she lifted up and pressed herself more fully against me.

And that's when I knew that I didn't care if this was a mistake.

Nothing this good—*nothing that felt this good*—could be a mistake.

I pulled away from her mouth, panting, and stared into her eyes.

"Are you sure?" I asked. "You've had a bad day."

She nodded. "Yes."

Yes. Nothing more, nothing less.

Just yes.

I lifted up onto my knees and pulled my t-shirt over my head, then followed up by hooking a hand around her jeans and panties at each of her hips, and yanking them down her legs.

Luckily, they came, because I hadn't bothered with the button.

One second they were there and the next, completely gone, leaving her bare to me.

The minute that her sex was exposed to me, I started to touch it with my free hand that wasn't gripping her thigh like my life depended on it, but she closed her legs, halting my progress.

"I have to tell you something," she murmured.

A dozen things soared through my brain. One, she was changing her mind. Two, there was something wrong. Three, she...

"It's been a really, really long time."

I halted in my tracks, my brain stalling on the words, 'really, really.'

"How long is 'really, really?'" I questioned slowly.

She sighed.

I reached over for the lamp, my hard cock brushing her upraised knee, and returned to my previous position on my knees beside her.

"Really, as in...never."

I blinked.

"You're not a spring chicken."

She nodded.

"And you're fucking hot."

She blushed.

"You're telling me that no one, not one single person in this whole goddamn world, has touched this?"

She nodded hesitantly.

I jerked off the bed and started pacing.

"I'm not a good bet," I repeated my earlier promise. "I'm fucking older than dirt. I've been with no less than fifty women in my time. I've been in prison for four years. I'm fairly sure that the minute I get inside you that I'm going to blow my load, and let's not forget that I'm six foot six. That means that I'm a big motherfucker. Everywhere. I'm not first-time material."

Out of all the things I expected her to do, laughing was not one of them.

But she did…laugh, that was.

At me.

She dropped her knees to the bed, and the move gave me a perfect view of everything she'd covered up, leaving me with my resolve wavering.

"You're so fuckin' funny." She brought her hand up to her eyes to wipe away the tears that were leaking out. "You think you're ever going to find a woman on Earth that is going to complain about a man having a big dick?"

I grunted, and then decided that there was nothing to do for it.

I had to show her what she was dealing with.

I'd always, and I do mean always, had to deal with the looks.

I'd had not one, not two, but four partners decline to fuck me after coming face to face with the monster.

Usually, a man wouldn't have a problem with being known as big, but once that shit was spread around, everyone looked at me funny.

It only took one girl to tell nearly all of the other high school girls, and then it was fuckin' over.

But having Kennedy understand that I wasn't fucking joking was paramount.

She needed to know that I was large and why this wouldn't work.

So I dropped my pants, and then shoved down my underwear to allow her to see it all.

My dick bobbed, the tip already weeping for her and everything she had to offer.

The laughter abruptly died, and she was on her knees within seconds.

"Wasn't fucking joking," I grumbled, letting her look her fill.

Her eyes came up to mine.

"I didn't think you were," she murmured, then hesitantly brought her hand up to wrap around my girth.

She swallowed thickly, then glanced up at my eyes before leaning forward.

Everything inside of me froze at seeing her mouth open.

Then, when her tongue met the head of my cock, I threw my head back and moaned.

Her other hand circled around my length right next to the other one, and she worked the length of my cock while she sucked on the tip like she'd done it a hundred times before.

"I've never done this before," she murmured, bringing her lips off the tip of my dick. "Is it okay?"

Then she blew on my cock...*fucking blew on it!*

And I felt the come boil in my balls.

"Hanging on by a thread here, woman," I choked out. "You do much better, and I'll damn sure go."

"Well, that doesn't sound like too much of a bad thing," she murmured. "How long does it take you to recover?"

Then she put her mouth on my dick again while she sped up her hand movements.

My legs started to shake, and I couldn't help but thread my fingers through her hair for something to hold on to.

I didn't hinder or help her movements, only laid them there, but the urge was definitely there.

If she wasn't so inexperienced, and I wasn't so much of a goddamn gentleman, then I'd yank her forward at the same time that I thrust.

She gagged, and I realized that maybe I wasn't so much of a gentleman after all.

"Fuck!" I moaned.

There was nothing hotter than watching her gag on my length.

At least, I thought that until she dropped both hands from around my shaft, then pushed forward, taking as much of me as she could physically fit into her mouth.

"Gonna come."

Three syllables were all I could manage, and when she still didn't come up for air while she practically choked herself on my cock, I realized that it was likely that she wasn't going to.

I felt it start at the base of my spine, swirling around my lower half, and then shoot out of my cock with so much ferocity that my knees went weak.

She didn't flinch away from me. Didn't stop her torture. Didn't do a goddamn thing other than take everything I had to give her.

She moaned around my staff at the first shot of come that left my cock, and the second. And the third.

By the time the fourth finally left, I was spent, barely hanging onto my feet.

She pulled away and licked her lips as if she'd just had the tastiest of treats, and then leaned back in the bed and scooted until her back hit the headboard.

"Come here," she whispered, patting the bed.

I did, practically falling face first into her lap.

If she could do that for me, then I'd return the fucking favor.

CHAPTER 14

Sweatin' like a hooker in church.
-T-shirt

Kennedy

He face planted in my lap, and I instinctively spread my legs so he wouldn't hit his nose on my ankle.

He caught himself before he could drop all the way down by planting both of his hands on either side of himself, lowering his body down much more gently than I was expecting.

But he used the opening of my legs to continue down until he was face-to-pussy with me.

"It's been four years," he told my vagina.

I bit my lip at the way it felt to have his breath touch my exposed lips.

Just the anticipation of his mouth anywhere near me was enough to have liquid need pooling at my entrance.

He turned his mouth and skimmed the prickly length of his beard against the inside of my left thigh. He drew it up until he came to the crease where my leg met my hip and then completely skipped over the one place where I wanted his mouth above all others and moved to the other side.

I closed my eyes and leaned my head back against the headboard, grinding the balls of my feet into the bed to stop myself from moving closer to him.

Then I felt the backs of his fingers moving slowly up the outside of my thigh, splitting my attention from what he was doing with his mouth to what he was doing with his hands.

I didn't know what to focus on, so I kept my eyes closed and just felt.

"You smell good," he said when his nose came to hover just over the top of my sex.

His hand circled around the outside of my thigh, then his arm hooked around it and pulled out, spreading me even wider.

His hand came to a rest just at the top of my sex, two fingers spreading the lips of my sex wide, and exposed my clit to his gaze.

"I bet you taste good, too."

Then he dipped his head forward and brushed the softest of kisses against the top of my clit.

It was only the barest of touches, but it was enough to cause my hips to jerk off the bed.

I'd never been touched by a man when it didn't involve clothing covering the majority of my body.

Never once had anyone but me touched myself there. Not in all my thirty years.

I was a complete and utter loner, and I found a chicken's company way more exciting than a human being's.

What Evander didn't know was that this—me being here, naked with him—was huge for me.

I was a massive loser who couldn't work up the courage to talk to a male gas station attendant, let alone a man who I would consider sleeping with.

But Evander made it easy.

He made it good.

He made it feel right.

I moaned out a sound that might've been some sort of word, but it came out sounding garbled and incoherent.

It was obviously something to Evander, though, because he leaned forward and took a swipe at my clit—this time with his tongue.

I bit down hard on my lip, trying to remain still while also feeling every single sensation that rushed through me at the rate of a million miles a second.

And when his lips slid down the lips of my sex, trailing down the center of me with just his tongue, I hissed in surprise.

I had no clue that it could feel that good.

I had no clue that anything could feel that good.

Had I known...

That thought came and went as I couldn't stand it any longer and had to bury my fingers in Evander's hair.

"I'm close," I panted, my hips now moving on their own volition.

He growled at me, then buried his face in my sex as he also buried his tongue inside of me.

I saw stars.

I also felt like I was on fire.

My thighs were trembling, my hips grinding against his face, and I was fairly sure that my heart was going to beat right the fuck out of my chest.

My hips were moving in time to his mouth, up and down and side-to-side.

But then his free hand smoothed up the back of my thigh and then skimmed over my sex, working me along with his mouth.

And then those talented fingers of his found me *there*—right where I needed something inside of me almost as much as I wanted my next breath.

The moment those fingers eased inside, I started to convulse.

My pussy clenched. My body bowed. My knees clamped down on his head like I was trying to crack a walnut with them.

And did I mention that I screamed?

I was an embarrassment to all of womankind.

All it took was minimal effort on his part, and I was putty in his hands.

If he asked for anything at that moment, I'd give it to him.

Why?

Because of orgasms.

Because I fucking loved him.

Oh, God!

I fucking *loved* him!

Before I could process much more than that, he was up on his knees, and I was up on mine.

He'd moved so fast!

One second I was on my back, staring at the ceiling, panting.

And the next I was bringing my knees up under me, and he was pushing inside of me.

I froze, half way up on my hands, as I waited for the pain.

And there was some, but not nearly as much as I would've expected.

But then he started to feed more into me, and I whimpered at the fullness.

I dropped down to my forearms and lowered my head to my fisted hands, saying a spontaneous prayer that I could take him.

He hadn't been lying.

He was big.

Bigger than the small vibrator I'd gotten off of Amazon three years ago. Bigger than the cucumber I'd once decided to play with when I was sixteen.

I wasn't a beginner when it came to dicks. I'd seen them before— in porn.

But Evander's was awfully big, and I wasn't going to lie about it being intimidating, because it was.

"Relax," he murmured, smoothing one large palm down my spine to settle on the small of my back.

I closed my eyes and tried to relax, sinking further into the mattress below me as I tried to will my vagina to allow him entrance.

But what helped more was his other hand at my hip that snaked around to find my clit, circling it slowly…methodically.

I moaned into my fist, biting the knuckle, as I started to rock my hips.

With each rock on my part, he sank in a little further in. And further. And further still.

I'd just decided that he should stop, once again getting uncomfortable, when he paused, and started to retreat.

Oh, good! I'd finally met the end of him.

But when he came back inside moments later, he didn't stop where he had before, but kept going.

I gasped, unsure that if I could take him, but then he pinched my clit, and I felt a jolt of electricity zip through me.

Each time I started to think I couldn't take any more of him, he'd do something with his hips or his fingers, and I'd forget for a few seconds that he was as big as he was.

And then he came to an end—either of me or him. I wasn't sure.

Whatever the reason he stopped, I wasn't complaining.

Maybe this sex thing wasn't all it was cracked up to be. Maybe if I…

He pulled out an inch, and ground himself back into me, making my heart skip a beat.

That felt good.

Really, really good.

Then he did it again. And again. And again.

Each time he moved those hips, something inside me started to build.

It started out small, almost inconsequential.

I could ignore it.

But as he continued, that tiny thing—that ball of need inside of me—started to grow.

One second I was praying for it to end, and the next I was pushing back against him, urging him for more.

More something...I didn't know what.

He obviously did, though, because moments later he was holding my hips as he thrust fully into me and then immediately pulled all the way out, allowing his cock to kiss the entrance to my pussy, before he slammed back inside.

It was then that I realized that I was taking not just some of him, but *all* of him.

His curly pubic hair was hitting my ass with each thrust and grind of his hips, and his balls were beating heavily against my clit.

My eyes were crossing as I started to pant, and as much as I wanted to move my hips in time to his thrusts, he held me immobile. Practically forcing me to take what he had to give and like it.

And oh boy, did I like it.

I liked it a lot.

Way more than I thought I would.

Then something inside of me snapped.

I cried out, Evander grunted in surprise at the force and speed of my orgasm, and I completely unraveled around him.

I lost my battle to stay upright shortly after that, falling flat to my belly.

Evander followed me down, and rocked his big body above mine, using me like only he could use me.

I felt his beard tickle my shoulder, and his sweat drip onto my neck.

Not once did I stop him, though.

Not only could I not, but I didn't want to.

Feeling that big body above mine was enough for the orgasm train to start pulling out of the station again.

And I likely would've accomplished another one had Evander not shuddered above me. His cock jerked, and I felt the hot splash of him filling me up, one jerk at a time, until he stilled completely.

Nothing broke the silence but our gasping breaths.

I could feel his hammering heart against my back, and I wanted to hold him tight.

My hands refused to work, however, leaving me laying underneath him while he worked up enough energy to roll over. Which didn't happen for at least two minutes.

"Goddammit," he groaned, moving with me, rolling me over with him, keeping us connected as he did.

I gasped as cold air met my overheated skin.

"You okay?" he rumbled, smoothing his hand down the middle of my chest.

I nodded against him, feeling my hair sliding down over my face and to his chest beneath me.

And that's about when I realized that this position wasn't very comfortable.

Overall, Evander was a hard guy. He had muscles on top of muscles, and although they were beautiful to look at, they weren't all that comfortable to lay on.

"What do we do now?" I asked, wondering if he cared if we got the bed messy.

Because I could feel it between my legs. It was pouring out around his cock now, which was quickly deflating inside of me.

Was it supposed to happen that fast?

Porn never showed that stuff…what happens after.

Should I get up and run to the bathroom? Should I grab for the sheet that I could feel around my ankle? What about my shirt?

I'd just about decided that my shirt would be the best option when he dealt with it for me, handing me a t-shirt—his—and ordering me to catch it as he lifted me by the hips.

I did, and covered not just me, but him as well. Except, by doing so, I also ended up grabbing him by the curlies, too, causing him to curse when he lifted me off of him.

"Oww!" he cried out, pausing midair in his attempt to unseat me from his cock. "You have my fucking hair down there in your iron grip."

I bit my lip to keep from laughing.

"If I let them go, you'll get your…errrm, stuff…all over you," I informed him. "I'm not any good at this yet."

He started to laugh, and then pushed me over to my knees, cursing only a few times as I practically ripped his pubic hair straight out.

"Jesus," he grunted. "Remind me not to do that again."

I would've laughed, really, I would have, but I was scared for the integrity of the shirt I was currently holding over my vagina.

"Ready for a shower now?"

He watched me, eyes resting for a few long moments at the shirt between my legs, before he nodded.

"Yeah. Probably should," he murmured. "I think I still have dirt in my hair. Another shower can't hurt."

The moment his big body was at my back, I smiled…and then led him to the bathroom.

Nothing had ever felt more right, yet so wrong, than they did right in this moment.

CHAPTER 15

Before coffee: Hates everybody.
After coffee: Feels good about hating everybody.

Evander

"So, are you ever going to tell me what you did to get a prison sentence?" she asked quietly.

I didn't want to talk about it.

But this was the first time she was talking in well over an hour without breaking out in a crying jag, and I'd do damn near anything to get her to stop doing that.

"Do you want to hear what they say happened, or what really happened?" I questioned.

She turned her head to stare at me, and I let my eyes roam over her face.

Her eyes were puffy from crying, and her cheeks were still wet from the most recent bout of tears that'd wracked her small body.

How someone as small as her could hold that many tears, and cry that hard, was beyond me.

I wanted nothing more than to throw my arms around her shoulders and pull her securely in to my chest, but I knew that she didn't need what followed me around like a black cloud.

I had the worst luck ever—hence, my prison sentence.

"Tell me what happened," she ordered.

I sighed, knowing that this was going to hurt, seeing the look on her face when she heard what I did to get a prison sentence, but I chose to tell her anyway.

It was better to get this out of the way now so I didn't get even more attached to her than I already was.

"I was driving home one night after work when I saw a woman walking down the side of the road."

She raised her brows at me.

"That sounds familiar."

I snorted out a gruff laugh.

"Yeah," I agreed. "Except, what I didn't know, was that she was a prostitute."

Her mouth dropped open.

"You...you picked up a prostitute?" she screeched.

I nodded.

"Saw a girl on the side of the road. Picked her up because she was in fucking heels, and I felt sorry for her," I mumbled. "It was dark, and she was on the main road that didn't even have a shoulder for her to walk safely on. Then, I realized that she was pregnant. So, I picked her up, and immediately got her to a shelter. I dropped her off and didn't think another thing of it until I arrived at work the next day to find the police there waiting for me."

"And what happened then?" she pushed, turning on the step to face me.

"I was arrested for the kidnapping and assault of the prostitute that I tried and failed to pick up the night before."

"But…wouldn't admitting that she was a prostitute send her to jail, too?"

I nodded. "Yes, and she got herself beat up while she was at it, too, so it could look all official and shit."

"And what? Did she have any witnesses?"

I nodded my head.

"One."

"And who was that?"

"The police chief."

Her mouth dropped open.

"Hostel's police chief?"

I grunted in reply. "The one and only."

"So the man in charge of all the police in our town is dirty?"

I nodded again.

"What about all the other police officers?"

I shrugged. "Don't know, and honestly, don't care."

"Why are you back?" she asked. "If they got you once, they can get you again."

I grinned then, showing my straight white teeth to her.

"I wasn't going to run and hide," I admitted. "Doing that would show the dirty bastard that he'd won, and I'll be damned if I give him that out."

She grumbled under her breath. "Did you figure out why she accused you of all that?"

I grimaced.

"There was a drug dealer down the street from here that always did his deals right outside my house. Him and another guy would pull onto my property and do their business at the end of my drive. I was pissed off that the little fucker kept doing his shit on my street, let alone in front of my house, so I beat the shit out of him and told him to move along," I murmured. "He didn't take too kindly to it, so he got one of his girls to play the damsel in distress card."

"And you fell for it, hook, line and sinker," she guessed.

I nodded. "I sure the fuck did."

"That doesn't sound right," she murmured. "There are checks and balances in the system to prevent this from happening."

"The so called 'system' failed me," I told her bluntly. "A cop could've done a little more digging and gotten to the bottom of it, but since what the detective found out fit me, and my background seemed to fit the situation, he didn't bother to look any further," I groaned. "I also couldn't afford a fucking lawyer, so I had one appointed to me. The only problem was that his wife was pregnant, and he didn't want to find a way for me to get off, because he kept comparing the prostitute to her—whether I did it or not, so he chose to slack off. I fired him and tried to represent myself, but that didn't go all that well either."

"So you served time for assault, robbery and kidnapping?"

I nodded. "Assaulting the pimp was never one of the charges against me. Apparently, he allowed me to go to jail as a punishment for beating the shit out of him since he knew that he couldn't take me in a fight. One that he knew I'd be willing to give him if he'd wanted it."

"So you beat the shit out of her pimp, two other guys that were with him, and were punished by going to jail for assault, kidnapping, and what...murder?"

"Not murder," he disagreed. "The detective did do something right. Found out that the prostitute had lost her baby the previous night in the ER. She was scheduled to have a D&C the next day."

All Kennedy could do was shake her head.

"And where was your brother during all of this?"

I grimaced. "That detective I was talking about?"

Her mouth dropped open in anger.

"He did not."

I shook my head. "No, the detective wasn't him. But he's best friends with him. You know that guy whose truck I recovered from Lowe's?"

She nodded, eyes wide.

"That's him."

"What a douche," she grumbled, still shaking her head. "You should find a better lawyer. You could get compensation. You could get money from the state for wrongfully convicting you and sending you to jail!"

I grunted. "Takes money, darlin'."

Her eyes filled with tears. "But that's not fair!"

I laughed humorlessly. "Didn't anyone tell you that life wasn't fair?"

Plus, I was doing something about it…just not through the legal system.

"Well, if I had money, I'd hire a lawyer for you. A private investigator, too."

I dropped my hand to her head and curled it around her neck before I pulled her to me.

"Don't get yourself caught up in this," I told her, mouth only inches away from her, making us eye to eye.

She narrowed her eyes, and I squeezed the back of her neck lightly.

"Trust me on this. With the chief of police, Fowler, being dirty, and that shitty Detective Mueller, you really won't get anywhere with this. Dumbass number one will fuck you over for a pretty penny, and Detective Mueller already dislikes you for having anything to do with me over him."

"Not to mention he's obviously a shit detective."

I shrugged at her words.

She wasn't wrong.

"Leave it be," I ordered her.

She looked away, but I turned her back to face me with my hand that was still on her neck.

"Promise me that you won't get involved in this," I said. "When I leave here…you need to leave it that way. You need to stay the fuck away from me and not look back."

Her face became thunderous.

"I'm not staying away from you just because there are dumb people in this town who don't know their assholes from their elbows."

I squeezed her neck and got up, grabbing my jeans from the floor.

After shrugging them on, I reached down to the floor for my socks and sat on the bed before putting them on.

"You're leaving?"

I didn't bother to look at her.

If I did something stupid like that, I might very well decide that I wanted to stay.

And I couldn't stay.

It was already bad enough that I'd fucked her—without a condom I might add.

Something so fuckin' stupid I couldn't even begin to count the ways.

"Yeah, I'm leaving," I told her. "Better for you if I'm not here."

She touched my back. "Will you come to me tomorrow?"

I finished putting on my socks and reached for my boots, dislodging her hand.

"I don't know that that is a good idea," I told her bluntly. "The more we're seen together, the worse things will get for you. If you need me, you can call. But no, I won't be here."

Which made me feel like utter shit.

But this was her life we were talking about. Her sister was dying, yes, but she had to go on living. And she had to keep doing it in this very town that was as corrupt as fuck.

So no, I wouldn't be putting her in any more danger than I already was.

My plans were already set into place.

And she wasn't a part of them.

Once I slipped my second boot on, I got up and walked out without another word.

I did stop once I made it out of her drive to call a contractor to come fix her roof, though. It wouldn't do to have her living in a place that was dangerous. I couldn't keep her safe from me by staying away and fix her house at the same time.

Time for plan B.

Lani Lynn Vale

CHAPTER 16

I love how fresh my bathroom smells when I kill a spider with an entire bottle of Febreeze.
-Meme

Kennedy

The day after Evander walked out, I was literally broken.

I was standing outside of my sister's hospital room, and I was looking in at my dad at her bedside, along with her three kids, my brother, as well as my brother-in-law.

They were all talking quietly around Trixie's bedside, and I wondered if I should even bother going in.

They'd obviously been there for a while.

Food was on the table in the corner, and there were three beds made up at the back of the room.

The kids were all sitting on the bed in the corner of the room, all of them huddled onto one cot, staring at an iPad that the eldest boy, DJ, was holding.

DJ was the first one to see me standing there, and the moment he did, his eyes lit up.

"Aunt Kennedy!" He handed off the iPad to his sister, Lucy, who discarded it, too, and started running toward me.

I dropped to my knee in the hallway and opened my arm as two wiggly bodies hit me with all the force that an eight-and-a-half-year-old and a four-year-old could muster.

The last one to hit me was little Jaxon, and he wormed his way in between his brother and sister and put his sticky hands on my neck and offered me a kiss.

"Where have you been?"

That was DJ, and his tone of voice sounded accusatory.

"I was told that visiting hours started at eight. I would've been here earlier had I known that I could, bud."

DJ looked into my eyes to gauge my sincerity.

"The doctors let us in here all night since mommy's sick."

My heart clenched.

"Are you okay, buddy?"

He nodded, but I could tell the only thing that was keeping him strong was the fact that his brother and sister were standing with us, rapt attention on his every word.

Not that the four-year-old, Lucy, or the three-year-old, Jaxon, really had any clue what was going on.

Likely, they never would.

One day, Trixie would be here and the next she wouldn't, and they'd never understand what happened.

"I'm here now, buddy. Have y'all had something to eat?"

My eyes went to Darren, who was practically glaring at me.

"No, they haven't had anything in a couple of hours."

I looked at Trixie, who was in the bed lying deathly still. "Do you…do you want me to take them to the cafeteria for a while?"

Darren's jaw clenched. "Yeah, that would be good."

I bit my lip and nodded, then turned my head down to stare at Lucy. "Do you want to go to the cafeteria and see what yummy food we can find? I hear they have awesome cookies!"

I had her at the word 'cookie' and knew it.

She nodded enthusiastically.

The girl was a cookie monster.

"Cookie!" she agreed. "Jax, do you want a cookie?"

Jax would do anything his brother would do, so I looked at DJ and raised my brows. "You want to go?"

He looked at his mother who was still in the bed, her face bruised, and her hands and arms covered in gauze. "Yeah, that would be okay."

I stood up from my kneeling position and held out my hand. "Let's go."

Jaxon and Lucy grabbed a hand, and DJ followed on the other side of Jack.

"You want to talk about it, buddy?"

DJ shook his head quickly, averting his eyes so that I couldn't gauge his honesty.

My stomach tightened even more.

"Did you make it to baseball last night?" I asked him, hoping to change the subject.

"Dad asked if I wanted to go…but no. I didn't. He was angry that I didn't, said I had an obligation to the team. But I didn't want to go."

I clenched my jaw. That'd been why I'd never gotten the call to take him. Go figure. Who would've thought to call the person that was waiting for your call and tell them that you no longer needed them?

"Did someone call your teacher to tell her that you wouldn't be there today?"

He shook his head. "No. Dad already got a call from the school for it, too. They said it would be an unexcused absence."

I stopped in front of the elevators and pressed the up button, stopping and turning to face him. "How about we call when we get to the cafeteria. I'll explain to them what's going on, okay?"

He looked relieved.

Darren and Trixie didn't put the same importance on school that most parents would.

Baseball, *yes*. The farm and doing chores, *absolutely*. School? *That would be a big fat no.*

Trixie and Darren barely graduated high school, and they felt that school, although a necessary evil, wasn't something that was crucial. Especially if there was farming business to be done or they needed the extra hand that DJ could offer.

How my sister got her nursing degree still baffled me. Then again, it baffled me that she didn't use it. *I would have.*

It was sad, really. Although farming was our way of life, I didn't think that it needed to be the way of life for *everyone*.

Hell, my own personal story of how my meager farming income was killed off—literally—in a little less than a few hours was proof enough that you should always have a backup plan.

Sure, I had gone to college and graduated with a degree in business, but I hadn't worked an office job with a boss in well over a half decade.

"Sounds good, Aunt Kennedy," he hesitated. "I'm glad you're here."

My face softened at the sweet boy's words. "I'm here if you need me. If you ever need me…just call, okay?"

DJ looked away before I could get a gauge on how he was really doing, but the small glimpse that I did see was enough to tell me that he wasn't doing anywhere near as well as he was making himself out to be.

Dammit.

I'd have to have a talk with Darren.

After this was all over. I'd have him keep an eye on DJ to make sure that things didn't get out of hand.

***

Turns out, the cafeteria did have amazing cookies. We all had two, and when the cafeteria workers got a load of Lucy's beautiful blue eyes, they gave her some hot ones from the back. And a glass of milk.

Everyone was a sucker for Lucy's blue eyes.

Hell, I was, too.

"Y'all ready to head back?" I asked as I gathered up our wrappers, napkins and cups and headed for the trashcan that was only a few feet away.

When I turned around, all three were still sitting there, shaking their heads.

"How about we run down to the gift shop…get something nice for mommy?"

That got a bunch of head nods, so that's what we did next.

Thirty minutes later, we were on our way back up to the room, when a nurse flagged me down.

I gestured for DJ to keep walking, thinking that it was something to do with Trixie.

"Head on down there. I'll be there in a minute."

DJ nodded, the big stuffed octopus in his hands as he lightly shoved Jack in the right direction.

I watched for a few seconds before turning at the sound of the woman's cleared voice.

"Ma'am?"

I turned, a smile on my face.

"Yes?"

Those kids made my heart happy, even when I was sad.

"Can you meet me on the other side of the station?"

I agreed, but held up a finger. "Let me make sure they get in the room all right."

She nodded thoughtfully, and I watched as Jaxon finally turned the corner to Trixie's room, and then turned on my heel and met the woman on the other side of the nurses' station, nearest the exit.

When I met her at the corner, right at the opening of the nurses' station, she started to wring her hands.

"I've been asked to explain to you that you're not allowed back inside the room while the family is there."

My mouth opened in surprise.

"What?"

She visibly winced.

"The family has requested that no visitors be allowed back until they say."

"But...but she's my twin sister."

The woman looked torn, but she held strong. "I'm so sorry."

Fucking Darren.

Why did he hate me?

If I was being honest, he'd always disliked me, and I could never figure out exactly why.

I was good enough to watch his kids. I was good enough to do things for him and help around the farm when he needed it.

"Are you okay?"

I looked up, not realizing that I'd dropped my head, and gave one firm nod.

"Yeah," my voice cracked.

"Are you sure?"

No, I wasn't okay. And no, I wouldn't be okay.

My sister was dying, and I'd never get to see her alive again because her husband was a douche bag.

"Will you...will you call me?" I asked, my throat thick and my hands clenched tightly.

Her eyes filled with sorrow.

"I will. The moment that anything changes, I'll give you a call," she hesitated before saying what she said next. "I'm not supposed to give you any information on her, but she won't make it through the night."

I closed my eyes for a few long seconds, then nodded once mutely. "Thank you."

My voice cracked, but I held strong.

I made it all the way to my truck, which thankfully had started today, before I broke.

***

Evander

I watched her cry.

I watched her cry for so long that I worried for her health.

Just when I was about to get out of the truck, she seemed to pull herself together and left.

I watched her go, then went on to the job I was supposed to be at over an hour ago.

CHAPTER 17

I run like the winded.
-T-shirt

Kennedy

Three days later

I was *pissed.*

It'd been seventy-two hours since Trixie had passed, and I hadn't heard word one from Darren the entire time.

I'd had to find out from the paper—*the fucking paper!* —when Trixie's funeral was. Too bad it was a day after the funeral.

I didn't even get to say goodbye!

Now I was at his house, wondering why the hell I was getting calls from the school saying that the kids transfer papers were ready.

"We're leaving," Darren said as he resituated the box that was tipping precariously over the top of the front seat. "Today."

"You're leaving?" I gasped, so surprised to hear Darren's words that they hit me like a physical blow.

"It's too hard on them to see you," he lied. "Looking at you is like a reminder, every day, that their mother isn't here anymore."

My mouth went dry.

"Darren," I paused. "That's not my intention, but when I saw them at the hospital, they didn't seem like that was bothering them. They seemed happy that I was there. What's really going on?"

He snorted, "Doesn't matter what you think. What matters is what is."

Fucking asshole.

"You're moving. What about the house? What about the land?"

He looked away.

"I sold it."

My stomach sank.

"You what?"

I couldn't believe what I was hearing.

He'd sold *our* family land? He'd sold the land that my father had given to him, thinking one day he'd give it to his kids.

"You seriously did not do that." I found myself biting my lip.

He looked away again.

"I had to have money to move away from here. Seeing you every single day is enough to make my heart hurt." He turned to look at me. "The sight of you makes me want to vomit."

I looked down at my hands.

I mean, on one hand, I could understand that by looking at me it had to be bringing up memories that were still too raw to touch on.

On the other, though, he'd known that Trixie and I were twins. He'd known how close we were—at least how close I thought we were. He'd known that that land wasn't just his. It was ours.

And now it was gone.

"Who did you sell it to?"

"A corporation," he said. "I'm not sure of their actual names. Listen, Kennedy."

I didn't want to look at him. I was afraid that if I did, then my carefully constructed wall that was keeping my tears at bay would crumble.

"The kids and I are leaving, and moving to Iowa, closer to my parents." He paused. "I want you to give us a while before you come visit."

"How long is a while?" I finally asked, voice rough and raspy with my need to cry.

"A year," he paused. "Maybe two. I'll let you know when it's okay."

A year or two.

Did he know that I saw those kids three times a week for hours a day for the last three years? Did he realize how hard it was going to be not to see them anymore? *They'd think that I abandoned them!*

But there was nothing I could do, so I nodded, sick to my stomach.

I didn't agree, but these were his kids. I had no right to tell him how to raise them.

"Thank you for understanding."

He started to close the door, but I stopped it by placing one hand on the side of the door. He could've slammed my hand in it if he'd wanted to, but I was betting he wouldn't.

"She was deathly afraid of that tractor."

Darren opened the door and glared at me.

"We let our insurance lapse." He said.

I didn't know what to say to that.

"We couldn't afford to pay it." His face completely closed down. "This way the kids get money from the state for losing a parent. If we'd have had to pay for her medical bills, we couldn't afford to live."

Then he closed the door, leaving me reeling.

I knew what he was saying.

They couldn't afford to pay for the cancer treatment. This way, she died with dignity. This way, she didn't suffer. This way…this way I lost my sister a whole lot faster than I would've the other way.

And just like that, he started the car—*my old car*—and drove away. It'd been mine when I was sixteen, and I'd given it to Trixie when hers had bit the dust a little over a year ago.

Then I'd taken on a car payment for the old blue beast that I drove around now.

Fuck my life.

One of these days I'd wake up from the nightmare that my life had become.

CHAPTER 18

I don't have to check the prices when I shop. I make my own
money and spend it how I want to.
-Me at the dollar store.

Evander

I went to her house three days after her sister had passed away. The funeral that I told myself I didn't need to go to, yet went anyway. Though I hadn't seen her there.

Why she hadn't been there was killing me.

What would keep her from that?

Needless to say, I needed to go check on her.

I had to figure out what was going on.

I didn't know what I was expecting.

One, I was expecting her house to be locked up tight. *It wasn't.*

Two, I was expecting her to be somewhere outside, tending to her animals. It was a routine of hers, one she was very meticulous about. *She wasn't.*

Three, I was expecting to find her raving mad and pissed off at the world. *That was the furthest thing from what she actually was.*

I found her in the bathroom.

Under water.

With a snorkel attached to her mouth so she could breathe.

It was surreal.

When men say that they love their wives and girlfriends despite their quirks, I don't think that Kennedy ever got the memo.

Love was weird.

I hadn't felt it before…not like this.

I'd loved my sister. I'd loved my dog. I'd adored my mother.

What I hadn't thought was that I would love Kennedy.

But despite the weirdness and the quirky traits, I did. I loved her. I loved the way she loved her niece and nephews. I loved the way she doted on her chickens like they were actual human beings rather than animals. I loved that she always blurted out random stuff that wasn't relevant to the conversation. I just loved her.

But I couldn't tell her that.

Just like I couldn't allow her to be more to me than what she was—a one night, one time, never going to do it again—stand.

Kennedy didn't know what I went through on a daily basis.

She didn't know the degree to which I was disliked in this small town.

She also didn't know that I had revenge in my soul, and the only way it was going to go away was when that corrupt asshole of a police chief got booted out of his office on his ass.

She only saw the good in me. The things that she wanted to see.

Because had she seen it all, she would know that she was in love with a man that had a very high likelihood of getting hurt.

I was nothing but bad news. I wasn't expecting my life to change anytime soon.

My brother, who was supposed to be my friend—*my own goddamned brother*—didn't even watch out for me.

I had a way of getting rid of the people that were supposed to mean the most to me.

But as I sat there and watched her through the water, all of my worries seemed to just…disappear.

It sounded cliché, like I was just making excuses.

But when it came to this woman, all of my carefully laid plans were shot to hell.

I reached my hand down into the bathtub, wincing when the hotter than hot water hit my hand, and kept going until I reached her foot.

Circling my hand around her ankle, I pulled her down the length of the tub until her legs were hanging over the side.

She came willingly, and it was then that I saw her eyes on me through her mask.

She was watching me watch her.

"What are you doing in there?"

She blinked, then shrugged.

I offered her my hand, and she took it.

The moment she was on the ledge of the tub, dripping wet, she said, "My head hurts."

"So you decided to submerge yourself underwater in hopes that it would stop?"

She looked away.

"Maybe."

A grin kicked up the corner of my mouth, and she turned around to glare at me.

"What?" I questioned, my eyes sliding down her still wet body. "You have steam coming off your body."

She tried to cover herself up better, but her arm could only cover so much of her boobs.

The other hand was at the apex of her thighs, covering up the thatch of hair that wasn't covered by the way she crossed her legs.

"What are you doing here?" she asked, hoping to take my attention away from my perusal of her body.

I ran a finger down the line of her jaw, and then up again to circle a strand of wet hair and tuck it behind her ear.

"Doing things that I shouldn't."

She bit her lip.

"Like checking on you to make sure you're okay."

Making sure that her roof was in good repair—which it was.

She looked down.

"Are you okay?"

When she didn't lift her head up, I did it for her by using one fingertip just underneath her chin.

"Look at me."

When she finally lifted her chin, I saw the tears that were forming in her eyes, and once again, my belly clenched.

It almost seemed like that was its usual state of feeling lately.

Every time I thought about the woman, it'd clench up tight.

"Why weren't you at the funeral?"

The first tear fell.

"He told me it hadn't been decided when it would be held."

Her breath hiccupped.

"And everyone looks at me like I'm some sort of a traitor now, since I didn't go."

I cupped her face with my hand and swept away the tear before it could make its track all the way down her face.

"That has nothing to do with your sister and everything to do with you hanging out with me in public," I told her honestly. "If you'd take time to listen to what they have to say, you'd hear."

She started to laugh.

In my face.

"I'll give you that," she agreed, wiping away another tear that spilled over. "But it wasn't all of it. Mostly, they're saying we're good fits since we both have brother/sister problems."

I snorted.

"My brother has always been standoffish when it came to me," I told her. "He had a mom and dad who loved him. I had a mom, and a dad that loved another freakin' kid. We all knew who my dad was, and we all knew who his choice was. To this day, there is still something between me and my brother, and it will always be there."

"That sounds…awful," she admitted. "How can people be so cruel? I thought you were supposed to love your kids?

"My dad met my mom, slept with her, while he was also 'courting' another woman," I explained, stepping back and pulling her wet body with me.

When she came, I lifted her up and placed her down on the counter, then went for the towel that was at her side.

With slow, methodical movements, I started to dry her off, starting with her toes and finishing with her hair.

"Apparently, the minute he won the other woman, he stopped seeing my mom. Only, he left a little something behind—that being me."

"I'm sorry, Evander."

I shrugged. "Doesn't bother me much anymore. Hurt like a motherfucker to see them when I was a kid, though."

"I'm sure," she said, then sighed. "I'm wallowing in self-pity."

He grinned.

"I'm here to take you out."

Her hand found my chest, and then smoothed down the length of my side until she came to my belt.

"I'd rather you just take my mind off of my worries."

I leaned in and pressed my mouth to her forehead.

"You don't want that."

I was hanging on by a thread.

If I distracted myself with how hurt and broken she was, then I could control my baser instincts.

But when she started talking like that, I found myself unable to keep focused on what I'd come here to do—and that was to help her.

I couldn't help her by fucking her.

At least, I didn't think I could.

Kennedy, obviously, had other ideas.

This I found out moments later when she hooked one hand in the belt of my jeans and yanked me forward.

The move put my cock up against the length of her now exposed sex.

The towel that I'd spread out over her body was now shoved to the side, and the only thing covering her up was the length of wet hair that was curling around her nipples—which were now playing peek-a-boo.

"I said, *take my mind off of it,*" she repeated. Slowly this time.

Fuck!

Out of everything, though, it was the intensity of her eyes that had me leaning backwards and unbuckling my belt.

"This isn't a good idea," I told her bluntly.

She shook her head. "Don't you know?"

"Know what?" I asked, pausing in my effort to loosen my belt.

"I don't care what everyone else thinks. I only care what you think."

Then she slammed her mouth down onto mine, making me temporarily forget what I was trying to do.

When she broke the kiss, her eyes were liquid pools of need.

"I care what everyone else thinks," I told her. "I don't want you hurt."

She reached for the hem of my damp shirt and lifted it up and off my shoulders.

The move left the shirt inside out in her hands, and she shook it out, then started to shift so that it was underneath of her.

"What's that for?"

She grinned.

"You've fucked me once, Evander," she said, shifting her hips so the shirt lay flat beneath her. "I know that you might start off all nice and slow, but you finish hard."

My dick hardened even further.

"And I don't want the skin of my ass getting countertop burns when I don't shift with your movements."

The shirt was a good idea.

Especially when I reached for both of her ankles and pulled her ass clear to the edge.

"Very good idea," I agreed.

Her smile was wicked.

"You're wearing too many clothes," she pointed out, lifting one eyebrow.

I winked.

"Am I?" I asked, circling one of her legs around my hips and pressing lightly for her to hold it there.

She did, and watched me as I brought my free hand up and trailed the pad of my thumb gently down the lips of her exposed sex.

She shivered, eyes on me.

I didn't know where to watch.

Her eyes? Her hard nipples? The way her chest was moving up and down with her increased breathing? The way that her sex seemed to shine with the wetness that was leaking out of her?

Fuck, but it was a lot to take in, and I wanted to see it all. *Taste it all!*

I lifted one of her ankles up and pressed a kiss to the inside of it before dropping it onto my shoulder.

With my free hand, I finished undoing my belt and then my jeans.

The moment that the confines were loosened, I pushed them both down my legs, and watched her eyes as she found my cock.

It was hard—so fucking hard that it hurt.

The head was a thick, ruddy red that looked angry, and the veins that were pulsing with blood were prominent and full.

She licked her lips.

"You going to stick that in me?"

I leaned forward slightly and let the head of my dick play along her slickened folds, up and down, coating first the head, and then my entire length, in her wetness.

When I glanced up, it was to find her head thrown back, wet strands of hair sticking to her skin.

Each time I let my tip slide against her clit, she would tense. Her nipples were hard as glass, and she was jerking, causing her voluptuous globes to jerk and jump with each of her movements.

Not paying any attention to erring on the side of caution, but instead only thinking about what it would do to me to feel her sweet heat enveloping me again, I slid my cock to her entrance and stilled.

My eyes closed of their own accord, and this time it was my head falling back as I slowly sank inside of her.

Only intending to give her an inch, I couldn't physically stop myself from giving her more when I felt her surround me—more and more and more until I was inside of her as far as her body would allow me. For now.

My eyes were clenched tight, and I was having a hard time drawing oxygen into my lungs.

Then I felt her nails dig into my thighs as she cried out, "Please!"

I probably would've managed to hold still—to give her the time she needed to adjust—if she hadn't started convulsing around me.

Seemed she didn't need the time, because just the act of pushing myself inside of her, and giving her my length, was enough to make her come.

Her pussy started to ripple, and I couldn't stop myself from pulling out, and slamming back inside.

I did this only twice before I realized, once again, that I really should be wearing a condom.

Really, I should be.

I knew that I was clean. I was about a hundred and two percent certain that she was clean, but that didn't mean that she was on birth control.

In this day and age, I was endangering her with my inability to control myself.

But I was blaming it on my dry spell. I was blaming it on Kennedy's virgin pussy that just begged for me to do bad things to it.

And if I was being completely honest, the idea of Kennedy swelling with my child would give   me the perfect excuse to stay. I could be with her and not feel guilt every time I turned the goddamn corner.

I'd then be with her for the sake of our child, not because I was selfish and wanted her there with me.

But I was fooling myself.

Fooling her.

And she wasn't stupid.

So before I could come in her, I pulled out and jacked myself off over her stomach, gasping when the first spurt of come decorated right below her breasts.

The second spurt went only an inch or so lower, pooling in the depth of her belly button.

The third and final spurt hit the trimmed curve of her lower lips, mingling with her desire and mine, making an attractive concoction that I couldn't quite help swirling my finger in, and bringing it up to her mouth.

The sexiest things I'd ever seen someone do were the things she'd done with me.

Come. Watch me. Change in front of me. Wash her fucking hair.

But watching her lick my finger clean of my release and hers was enough to top the list of my all-time sexiest things list.

"Fuck me," I growled, eyes dilating and hands clenching.

My cock was still throbbing with my release, and Kennedy's chest looked flushed with desire.

And I probably would've dropped down and given her my mouth, but my phone rang.

"Shit."

She moved to stand, and I backed up, giving her room.

Then she went for the towel, picked it up, and wiped herself clean while I reached for my phone.

"Hello?"

CHAPTER 19

I may not be a Victoria's Secret model, but I could pick one up and squat her.
-Kennedy's secret thoughts

Evander

"Hello?"

"Meeting started five minutes ago, where the fuck are you?"

That was Travis, and he didn't sound happy.

"Ran into a problem," I said, eyeing Kennedy. "I'll be there in fifteen minutes."

Travis muttered something and hung up, leaving me standing there, my pants around my thighs, staring at Kennedy as she cleaned herself of my release.

I watched her drop the towel, and then walk out of the room, but only far enough that she could get to the bed and flop down on it, face first.

My lips twitched.

Buckling my pants up, I walked into the bedroom and stood over her.

"Come on," I ordered, hauling her up from her sprawled position by one ankle. "I have a company meeting, and I need to run by my place and change. And I would like to take my bike because it's a beautiful fucking day out, and we needed to be there about five minutes ago…that okay?"

She stood shakily on her feet, and her face was a mask of pleased tiredness. The look on her face, paired with what we'd just done, was enough to make me feel smug.

"Yeah," she said. "I'll ride on your motorcycle with you. What should I wear?"

I thought about that for a moment.

"You have any leather?"

She didn't really need leather. More so she just needed pants, but I'd love to see her rounded ass in leather.

Not that the stuff she wore wasn't extraordinary enough, but the thought of seeing those rounded curves in something that was so tight on her ass that it was like a second skin—yeah, that did things for me.

Things that shouldn't be happening when I'd just had her, but oh well.

It was what it was.

"I have a leather skirt," she said. "But no leather pants…which would be the only thing I would wear on a motorcycle. I've seen some crazy Facebook video footage of what happens when a woman wears a skirt on a bike."

I grinned and pulled her to me.

"Yeah?" I asked. "What happens?"

"People get a sneak peek whether the skirt-wearer wants them to or not."

My gut twisted.

"Wear pants," I grumbled.

Her lips twitched. "Yes, Sir."

***

Twenty—not thirty—minutes later, we pulled into the driveway of Hail Auto Recovery.

Instead of going inside like one would expect, I grabbed hold of Kennedy's hand and tugged her along behind me, taking her not to the shop, but to the club next door.

"What's this?" she asked, eyeing the club.

It was one of the most popular places in the area and owned by Travis and Dante Hail.

"I didn't realize that a city limit sign could be in the middle of a city."

I looked over at where she was pointing, and saw the sign that read Jefferson, Texas City Limits. Population: 4, 206.

"There's a story there," I said distractedly as I walked up to the door, grabbing Kennedy's hand as I did.

Atticus saw me, nodded his head, and then opened the club's door without another word.

We walked inside into a dark, quiet hallway.

"Well, are you going to tell me this story?" she teased.

I grinned.

"Hostel used to be a dry town, and when we decided to open the club, Hostel's city council flat out refused to allow them to have a liquor license. So they built the club—they, as in the owners, Travis and Dante—the next town over since they would approve the liquor license. That's Jefferson, Texas."

"Was the garage always there?" She pointed behind her, I assumed to indicate the Recovery shop.

"No," I said. "When the business took off, they rebuilt it. But they wanted it in Hostel, and not Jefferson, because that's where it was established. In the beginning, Dante and Travis, as well as Dante's wife, started it out of their garage in Hostel. For a short time, they moved to Louisiana and opened another branch in Shreveport, but they no longer run that location. Though, the location still uses 'Hail Auto Recovery' for the name because it's an established business there."

"Sounds confusing," she murmured, stopping when we came to a door.

I pushed it open, and the pulsing sounds of the club started to vibrate around us.

"Wow," she gasped. "I've never even heard of this place. It's amazing."

I laughed. "The way you tell it, your sister's the one who took you out and got you to see new places and things. You're not really the type to go out and party. I can see why you wouldn't know about this place."

I immediately felt badly about mentioning her sister, and the frown and sadness that entered her eyes was enough to make my heart clench.

Fuck!

Then she smiled.

"My sister tried to get me to go out with her once to a club downtown, but I flat out refused. It's not surprising that she wouldn't tell me about this one."

I squeezed her hand and tugged her into me, wrapping my arm around her shoulder as I directed her into the back of the club, down a long hallway, and into the private quarters that the Hail crew, also known as the Hail Raisers, occupied when they were in the club.

The moment I pushed open the door, Travis, who was on the front of the table leaning against it with his feet crossed, stood up.

"Fucking finally."

"Sorry," I muttered. "This is Kennedy. Kennedy, that's Travis. I'll introduce the rest to you once we're through with the meeting."

I'd do it now, but Travis looked fucking pissed that I was late.

Eyes wide, Kennedy nodded. "Okay."

It was how she moved closer to me that erased the scowl off of Travis' face.

The moment he saw that Kennedy was intimidated, he sighed and stood from his lean, offering his hand to her.

"Nice to meet you, Kennedy," he said, eyes intense on her. "Have a seat. This won't take long."

I walked to the closest two open seats, which happened to be at the end of the table, and took a seat.

Kennedy sat in the rolling chair and scooted up as close to the table as her chair allowed, and then placed her hands gently in her lap, waiting.

I grinned, and then took the seat beside her, not scooting up like she did, but scooting back so I could plant my feet on the table.

"Like hell it won't take long," Baylor grumbled, extending his feet into the chair beside him. "We need to figure this shit out before it gets too far out of hand."

Baylor was a Hail—an actual Hail, and not just a man that worked for Hail Auto Recovery.

"Agreed." Reed stood up and started pacing.

Reed was also a Hail. He was military—home for a few days from what I'd heard—and he had a bad attitude that nobody wanted to get near. Although others may know why, I didn't.

I studiously avoided everything that had to do with him seeing as I wasn't the touchy feely type and didn't want to find out why the fuck he was acting like a complete asshole.

Because asking people why they're sad, or angry, or anything really, invited more talking on their part. That was something I wasn't willing to deal with at this point.

"We can talk about Dante some other time, boys," Travis snapped. "He'll hold."

I wasn't sure that was true.

It had taken Travis a few weeks to explain exactly what was going on with Dante, but once he had, I'd immediately understood why he wasn't there anymore.

His wife and children had been killed in a car wreck—a car that Dante's sister had been driving.

And within weeks of that happening, Dante's sister, Amy, had killed herself because of her distress.

So yeah, I didn't need any further information on that front.

I could see why Dante would want to check out, and as long as he wasn't hurting the business, then I didn't see a goddamn reason in the world why everyone couldn't leave him the fuck alone.

His brothers, obviously, had different ideas.

I leaned back and sighed, wondering why exactly I had to be here for a meeting like this.

There were a hundred different things I could be doing right now.

Cleaning up my yard. Picking up a skip. Fucking Kennedy.

None of those things could be accomplished here.

"Fine," Reed grumbled. "But don't think that I won't beat the shit out of you if you keep avoiding me."

My lips twitched.

Reed was big, like Travis, but he was also about fifty pounds heavier and tolerated less bullshit.

It'd be an interesting fight, that was for sure.

"I have a new high-bond recovery, and I want to go over it before I assign it."

I was only halfway listening, my eyes studying the long strands of hair that were curling around Kennedy's neck, when I heard the name and froze.

"Balthazar Montes." Travis' eyes flicked up to meet mine the moment he said the name and watched closely as my fists clenched.

He knew who he was to me. He knew that that man was no bigger than a piece of shit and someone that I would love to run over with my truck if I ever had the chance—even if I had to drive through the gates of Hell to get to him.

"I'm sure some of you are aware of who he is…" Travis continued.

Everyone in the entire room was aware of who Balthazar was and what he'd done to me. What he'd taken away from me.

Luckily, nobody said a word as Travis explained why Balthazar was getting his car repossessed. My hope was that it was due to him being a complete moron.

My luck was never *that* good, though.

"Two people will take this skip," Travis continued. "If you need help, or see it in town, don't approach unless you have enough manpower. This asshole is dangerous and carries a shit ton of muscle with him everywhere he goes."

I knew that. That'd been the reason I hadn't approached.

It'd been the reason that little piece of trash wasn't lying dead in an alley somewhere far, far away from here.

"Understood?" Travis confirmed.

There were a few grumbled yesses from the men and a "Yes, fucking Sir," from Reed, even though Reed didn't normally take skips. See, Reed was actually a doctor—an OB/Gyn, in fact. It was rare that he was in town, and even rarer that he would take a skip. I had a feeling that the only reason Reed was here was due to whatever was going down with Dante.

Travis shot him a glare, and Kennedy started to giggle.

Causing me to smile.

"Shh," I whispered. "Travis is in a shit mood lately."

Her eyes turned my way, wide and surprised because she knew damn well that Travis could hear every word we said.

"I think now's the time we talk about hiring more people," Baylor piped up, ignoring Kennedy's giggling. "Without Dante here to help and Tate Casey in jail for the next three years, we need to hire more manpower."

My brows rose.

That was news to me.

I'd wondered where Tate was the last few weeks I'd been working again, but I hadn't had enough time to ask any of them where he was. I'd just thought he was on vacation.

He did that a lot. Sometimes he was gone for months at a time while he rode off into the sunset on his bike, and then he'd show up a month, sometimes two, later wearing a much happier smile.

"What the fuck is he in jail for?" I barked, leaning forward.

All eyes turned to me.

"Shit," Travis said, scratching his beard covered chin. "I thought you would've heard."

I shook my head. "Nobody talks to me anymore. They think I'm scary."

That earned another giggle from Kennedy, and I wrapped my hand around her ponytail and tugged lightly.

"Quiet, woman."

She didn't turn to me, but I could see the small smile on her face.

"He was making a pick-up two blocks from the club and drove up on a couple gang members raping a woman. A girl, really. You know how he is about that."

I winced.

Tate Casey was the gentlest man you'd ever come upon…unless it involved females.

Nobody knew the full story, but we'd all seen the light switch on in his brain over the years that we'd been working with him.

There was this one time, while we were doing a recovery together that had gone late—later than we expected, anyway—and we'd been there when the couple had arrived home.

Since we'd been in an area of the yard with our lights off that was fairly deserted, they didn't see us as they pulled in. Further, they didn't see us at the back of the lot as they opened the trunk of their car and yanked a little girl out.

A girl who'd been kidnapped earlier in the day.

And that same light had gone off in Tate's eyes as I'm sure had when he'd seen that girl being raped by the gang members.

"Goddammit," I rumbled, standing up and putting my hands on my head. "How long is he in for?"

"He got eight years, but due to his…errm…circumstances, he got a lighter sentence. Something much lower than he could've gotten for beating two teenagers to death. He has the possibility for parole in three years. My guess is that he'll get it."

I looked at Travis, knowing that he knew more than the rest of us. But I didn't press. If he wanted to share, he would have. Whatever he knew, it must've been big, because the guys in this office were a bunch of gossips. You couldn't keep a secret in this place to save your life.

"Well, fuck," I said. "That fucking sucks."

"I'm open for suggestions on hires if y'all have any," Travis groaned. "Goddammit, I'm tired. This shit is for the birds. Dante used to handle this part of the operation. All I had to do was drive a truck when I was needed and do the fucking taxes on time."

I thought about people that I knew who were up for the crazy, and sometimes life threatening, job of an auto recovery agent, and I could only come up with one man.

"I know one man. He's here for the next six months for some operation—which I'm not privy to so don't fucking ask—and then he'll be gone. But he used to be in the Army with me, and he's a good man."

"Who?" Travis asked.

"The dark, creepy motherfucker who I've seen hanging around the club lately?" Reed questioned, perking up at hearing someone that someone was around to help out, which would give him more time to visit his lady who was hours away where his other brother, Tobias, lived now.

I grinned. "That's him."

"Ask him," Travis ordered immediately. "As long as the two jobs don't interfere with each other, that's perfectly fuckin' fine."

"I know a SEAL…well, an ex-SEAL…named Brock," Baylor started. "I might have to dig him out of the bottle first, but he's around."

"Ask him," Travis said. "I'm not being picky at this point. I'd ask Mom and Dad to get some fuckin' sleep at night at this point."

I snorted.

Travis grinned.

Tobias and Baylor started to laugh.

Kennedy looked at me in confusion.

"Travis' parents are the sweetest, kindest people in the world. They fronted Dante the money to start this business fifteen years ago—when he was just twenty-five—but they'd never be able to take someone's car away from them," I explained to her.

"Ahhh," she nodded in understanding. "Got it."

I winked at her.

"Who is this Brock guy?" I asked Lincoln. "I saw someone at the diner the other day. He ordered a beer with his breakfast, and I think he was the only other person in the entire place who could take some of the heat off of me the entire time I was there."

Baylor nodded. "Was with me in the SEALs. Something happened. Something bad. He was looking for somewhere to go and I offered him up Hostel. He's staying in an apartment in Jefferson, though. The rent's cheaper there."

"All right, then ask those two. We will see how the workload lightens up and go from there," Travis scratched his head. "Did we go over the numbers for last month?"

"No," all of us said.

The numbers from last month were pretty much made up from what we pulled in with repossessions. Usually, there was a running count to see who could get the biggest payout, but I guessed that it'd taken a back burner when Dante's family had been killed.

And my guess was confirmed moments later when Baylor spoke.

"No point," Baylor sighed, his head tilting forward as he stretched out his neck. "I'm exhausted, and the faster I can get home, the faster I can get to fuckin' sleep."

Before Travis could reply to this, his phone rang, and he halted everything to answer it.

I understood why he'd done that moments later when he stood up like he had somewhere to be.

Which, I might add, he sure as hell did.

"Hannah's in labor. Gotta go." He paused at the door and looked at Baylor. "Assign that to whomever wants it and get to the hospital."

Baylor had already been halfway to standing when he got the directive.

"10-4," Baylor grumbled. "I'll be there. Good luck, brother."

Travis visibly shook himself and then he was gone.

"This his first kid?" Kennedy asked in surprise.

"No," everyone around the table answered at once.

The single word was said so abruptly, and with so much anger, that Kennedy shrank back in surprise.

"I think I sense a story," she murmured, this time for only me to hear. "But tell me later."

Baylor grunted, and Kennedy's faced flushed with the realization that she hadn't whispered quite as low as she thought she had.

"There really is nobody to give this to but you, man," Baylor handed off the file folder by sliding it across the table. "We gotta get to the hospital…just be smart, yeah?"

I lifted my lip in a silent snarl.

"I'll be smart," I lied.

I wouldn't be smart.

This was the ticket that I'd been waiting for. The entrance to the private Montes compound that had security that rivaled Fort Knox. The place that housed one of the two men who'd been responsible for leaving me to rot in that shit hole for four years.

Yeah, I wasn't going to be smart. I was going to kill that motherfucker with my goddamn bare hands.

And I had a good damn reason to be there.

Fuck. Yeah.

With the rest of the group leaving, it left Kennedy staring at me in anticipation.

"I have so many questions!"

I started to laugh as I pulled her up from her chair.

Once we got outside, I opened the truck door, but she waved it away.

"No, let's go over there and get some candy."

"Candy?"

"Candy!" She said, then started across the street to the gas station.

I followed behind her, eyes on her ass, and almost missed the woman who pushed out of the gas station at the same time Kennedy pushed in.

"I'm sorry." Kennedy apologized.

I looked up at the same time that I saw the vet staring at me accusingly.

"Dog stealer."

I gritted my teeth.

"What are you talking about?" Kennedy questioned Layne.

Layne turned her angry gaze to Kennedy.

"He didn't tell you that he stole my dog?"

Kennedy's eyes turned understanding.

"From what I hear, he didn't steal the dog. You were housing the dog, and he had a signed contract." Kennedy corrected her.

Layne didn't have anything to say to that. She flipped us both off and left, walking out of the gas station parking lot and next door to her clinic.

But she'd done the damage that she'd set out to accomplish. How, you ask? The town gossips had been standing in the middle of the parking lot next to a large Suburban. Three women, six kids, and two fathers that also helped coach the team that my nephew was on. All of the adults were staring at us with various degrees of disgust on their face.

Just fucking perfect.

"Let's go." I ordered, grabbing Kennedy's hand.

She tugged it away from me and went into the store. I stayed where I was, torn between following her and standing my ground.

I decided to stay and stare the group down, but two of the women were already on their phones, texting.

Just fucking great.

"Ready."

I looked down at the bag that Kennedy was holding.

She didn't have just a candy bar. She had six. Two half gallons of ice cream—Rocky Road and vanilla. And a huge rainbow popsicle the size of a 6-cell Maglite.

And as we walked away, she was sure to glare at each of the adults that she passed. Grabbing onto my hand and holding on for dear life as we made it back to my truck.

CHAPTER 20

Like a good neighbor, stay over there.
-Kennedy's secret thoughts

Kennedy

I rolled over in the bed, stared at the dented pillow, and frowned.

What had woken me up? Was it Evander leaving? Was he coming back? *He said he was going to stay...*

I threw the covers off, knowing that my mind wouldn't shut off until I knew for certain if he was in the house, and started out the door of my bedroom—without, might I add, putting on pants.

Which was my first mistake.

My second mistake was assuming that Evander was the only one in my house.

I heard murmuring from somewhere in the living room/kitchen area and assumed that either he'd gotten a call or he'd needed to make a call.

My guess was he'd gotten a call.

He got calls a lot.

I was surprised to know how many people had Evander's number.

At first, it was only the guys from work calling him, or the dispatcher calling with a pick-up for him to do.

Then, Evander explained, as his feelers started coming back and word got out that he was back, the low-life citizens of Hostel had started to call to give him tips. I wasn't quite sure why he was gathering the little snippets of information or what he was going to use it all for until he'd explained it to me.

Now that everyone in town knew he was back in the area, all the people who used to act as his informants—telling him, for a fee, where he could find the people he was looking for and when— were calling with leads, hoping to restart their previous relationships. He needed these people who knew things that Evander couldn't find out on his own without immersing himself in that world. A world, he'd explained, he didn't want any part of if it meant that his parole could be broken and he'd be sent back to jail.

My third mistake of the night was walking right into the living room without pausing to first make sure that the front freakin' door wasn't open.

At first, they didn't notice me.

At first, I didn't think about the chill of the cool night air hitting my skin where they should have been covered by my pants.

Why?

Because there was a large man covered in head-to-toe black— black jeans, black motorcycle boots, black t-shirt, and a black ball cap covering his black hair—and he was arguing with Evander.

"I can't do this for you," the man stated vehemently.

"You mean, you won't do it for me," Evander countered the man's obviously emotional refusal.

The man shrugged.

"I won't do this for you," he amended. "But it's not because I'm not willing to help. It's because I don't want to see you go back to jail all for some petty revenge that won't serve any real purpose and will barely get the man at the top of the food chain a fucking slap on the wrist."

Evander's back straightened. "You don't know that."

The man nodded his head. "I do. It may not happen the way I think it will, but it definitely isn't going to go the way you think it will, either."

Evander growled and started to pace from side-to-side in the small entranceway.

"He stole four years of my life, Rafe."

The anger and hurt in those words were enough to make my belly clinch.

"I know, man," Rafe said. "But he's going to steal more if you don't watch what the fuck you're doing."

Fear started to curl into my belly.

What could he be doing that would have this man—an obviously badass, all-black-wearing kind of guy—telling him that what he had planned wasn't smart? Evander wasn't a dumb man, not at all. Everything he did was intentional. He was the type of man who stopped to think first—and did so carefully—before he acted.

He weighed the pros and cons of his actions, considering every possible outcome and scenario, before he did anything.

Acting impulsively wasn't in Evander's nature, and if this man, Rafe, was thinking he was being impulsive, he was wrong. Whatever he had planned, it had been thought out thoroughly.

Whatever it was, though, it was obviously something bad.

I bit my lip and shifted my hip so I could get a better look, which caused the man in the door to look up and stare at me.

"She's up."

Evander stopped pacing and turned to look at me, eyes wide and wild.

"Jesus fucking Christ, Kennedy," he growled low in his throat and started to stalk toward me. "You're not wearing any goddamn clothes!"

I looked down at my pantless state, and then frowned, reaching for the afghan that was on the couch.

Before I could get it up, Evander was there, shrugging off his shirt and then pulling it on over my tank top, smoothing it until it covered me from mid-forearm to right above my knees.

"What are you doing awake?" he snapped.

I blinked.

Evander snapping—at me or even just in general—was foreign to me. I wasn't sure I'd ever actually seen him angry.

But this man, the one standing in front of me right this very moment, wasn't the same man I was used to. This man was angry, vindictive. This man was unforgiving.

"I woke up, and you weren't there," I whispered, tears automatically forming in my eyes.

And just like that, all the anger and annoyance drained out of Evander. In its place was a man who looked practically defeated.

"Head back to the bedroom. I'll be there in a minute."

I would've argued. Really, I would have. But the look on Evander's face brooked no room for argument from me. *At all.*

I could tell that with just one glance in his eyes.

"Okay," I finally murmured. "I'll just go do that."

Then I started backing away, watching as Evander watched me, until I hit the mouth of the hall.

The moment that I was out of sight, I turned and walked back down the hallway.

The murmuring didn't start up again, and that was either due to them going outside so I couldn't accidentally overhear their conversation again or the departure of Mr. Mysterious, the all-black-wearing, midnight visitor.

But while I waited, I quickly realized that something was very, very wrong here.

Evander was worried.

And I only had to listen to him twenty minutes later as he explained why, exactly, he should be.

Once he was through explaining everything to me, I was worried, too.

***

Evander

I saluted my former squad member—the man who had my back when Gertie wasn't there to do it—and closed the door quietly.

I shouldn't have bothered.

I knew that she was still awake, and likely on the edge of her seat waiting for her answers.

Answers that I didn't want to give—not yet at least, and, if I had my choice, not ever.

But I was a man who knew when his woman wasn't going to be appeased by some bullshit explanation.

I knew that she wouldn't stop until she got the answers she sought.

So I chose to share the details with her on the man who we'd gotten the repossession notice for earlier at the club.

I wasn't surprised to find her wide awake and waiting for me as I walked through her bedroom door.

I also wasn't surprised to see Gertie in the bed with her, legs sprawled out and his face in her lap. Kennedy's dog was also in the bed with them, stretched out by her feet and chewing on a piece of rawhide.

If anything good had come from all of the shit that happened and that was now my life, it was what I had in this woman.

Would I have met her had I not gone to prison? Would I be standing here, staring at her in this bed as she was petting my dog, if the nightmare I went through had not happened?

No, I didn't think so.

And it was tearing me apart inside.

On one hand, I wanted vengeance. I wanted Balthazar and the chief of police to fucking suffer. I wanted them to die, and I wanted them to die slowly. Painfully. Agonizingly.

I wanted them to feel it, every single second, as they died.

I wanted them to realize that I was not someone they could shit on and not give a second thought to. I was an opponent who was going to just roll over and let them play their stupid fucking games.

"Are you going to tell me what's going on?" she whispered.

Instead of sitting on the bed, I took the chair that she had piles of clothes sitting in, shoving them backwards so I was on the edge of the seat.

"Do you know who that was?" I asked.

She had to have seen him around town.

This wasn't a big town. Plus, I'd mentioned him while we were at the meeting today, and the types of places that he liked to frequent.

She nodded.

"Rafe?"

I confirmed with a nod of my head. "The one and only."

"Okay," she hesitated. "Then why was he here in the middle of the night, and what was he refusing to help you with?"

I paused, considering my words very carefully.

"The job that Travis gave us before he left today. I was asking Rafe for the help and offering him the job if he wanted it."

"And did he take it?"

I shrugged. "Yes, for a while, anyway."

"Then what was the problem?"

"He didn't want to help me catch Balthazar." I refused to keep her in the dark about what I was going to do in the next week. She deserved to know that I might fuck this up—just like Rafe said. "He wasn't refusing to help do the job as much as he was refusing to help *me* do the job."

She waited, eyebrows raised in question, for me to elaborate.

"Balthazar is the man who lives down the street from me," I said. "The one who didn't take kindly to me threatening him with the police. The one who's responsible for my four-year prison sentence."

The moment she realized who he was to me, and it sank in, her face fell.

"You can't do that job." She sat up straight, displacing Gertie's head. "If you do that, you could get hurt. You could go back to jail if you do what I think you're going to do. And where would that leave me?"

I gritted my teeth.

"I won't go to jail, and I won't get hurt."

She sat forward.

"You don't know that," she snapped. "You're so far from rational about this that you can't see what everyone else does, and that's that this is a bad idea. I mean, really, Evander, what are you thinking?"

What was I thinking?

"I'm thinking that if I don't do this, that stupid motherfucker is going to be a thorn in my side for the rest of his life. I'll have to deal with him doing his business at the end of my road, living with just a few acres separating him from me, and there wouldn't be a goddamn thing I could do about it."

"Your brother…"

I immediately shook my head.

"Not happening," I immediately disagreed. "He's not been there at all for me in a long time. I'm not bringing him in on this."

She growled under her breath and looked away as angry tears started to form in her eyes.

"This is the worst idea—it's not like you."

"You don't know it's not like me." I stood up and threw my hands in the air. "That's the problem we have here. You don't know me, Kennedy. You only know what you want to know."

"What do you mean I don't know you?" she hissed, standing up now, too. "I know you!"

I crossed my arms over my chest and stared at her, trying not to think about how hot she looked when she was pissed.

"You don't," I countered.

She stalked toward me, finger raised and poked me in the chest at the same time she said, "I know that you love me."

I snapped my mouth closed.

I did fucking love her.

I wouldn't admit that, though.

Admitting it meant that she'd just have one more hurdle to jump over when this all turned south.

And I wasn't lying to myself. This very well might turn south. I might end up back in jail after I did what I had to do. I might be fucking dead.

But there wasn't a goddamn thing that was going to stop me from exacting this revenge. My heart couldn't live with it, and if she really loved me, she wouldn't ask me to.

Until this was all over, I wouldn't say those words to her. I wouldn't give her the false hope.

So I remained silent.

And broke her heart in the process.

It's too bad that I didn't realize that I was breaking her heart while I was doing it, though.

"I'll see you in the morning," I said, taking a scat on the bed and dragging my boots to me.

"You're going tonight?" she asked in alarm.

I nodded, slipping my feet into the boots and standing up.

"Don't do this, Evander," she pleaded. "This isn't a good idea. I have a bad feeling about this."

I walked to her and hugged her, dropping a kiss on the top of her brow.

"I'll be fine."

Then I let her go.

"I love you, Evander."

My heart swelled at her words, but I didn't let them stop me from leaving.

But I really should have.

She looked just fine.

She looked like she was okay with me not saying it back to her.

As I got to the end of the sidewalk, though, I couldn't stop myself from turning around and heading back up the stairs.

She looked so fuckin' hopeful that my steps faltered.

"Gotta get Gertie," I rumbled. "Gertie!"

Gertie was at the door moments later.

And as I turned to leave, I got a good look at her face.

I saw the moment it fell.

Saw the resignation and hurt there.

I promised myself that I'd make it up to her. I promised myself that I would tell her everything. Show her everything that was in my heart.

As soon as I got home.

But when I got home would be too late.

I just didn't know it yet.

***

"Worst fuckin' idea, ever," Rafe grumbled, watching the house.

I watched it, too.

I'd done this a lot. Sat here, watching, waiting, hoping that Balthazar would come out so I could get my chance and grab the fucker.

But he never came out. I didn't know if he knew I was out there. I also didn't know if he would even care.

I'd done this before. I knew what I was about to do was stupid.

But then I got a phone call.

And what was said sent shock straight through me, right to my core.

"Hello?" I answered.

"You don't happen to know why I have three goats and a dog tied up outside the police station with a note to me on it, do you?"

That was my brother.

"What?" I was confused.

"A dog. Three goats. Tied to my cruiser."

My brows furrowed.

"What does the note say?" I asked distractedly.

I honestly didn't know why I would care whether he had a dog and three goats tied to his cruiser.

"Got a note. From your woman."

My heart froze.

Now I cared that he had a dog and three goats tied to his cruiser.

"How do you know it was my woman and why would she have anything to do with that?" I asked, sitting up straighter.

Not comfortable having this conversation in the car with Rafe, I pulled the door handle and bailed out of the truck, heading to the tailgate so I could lean against it.

"Because the note is signed 'Kennedy'," he drawled. "How else would I know they belonged to her?"

A sick feeling of dread hit me.

She wouldn't leave…would she?

"What did the note say?"

"Nothing that I'll be sharing with you," he shot back. "Get here and get these goats. I live in a fucking subdivision. I won't be able to do anything with them."

Then he hung up, leaving me staring at the fence of my worst enemy.

Knowing that I wouldn't be going in there today.

Not today and maybe not ever.

Not if it meant losing Kennedy.

CHAPTER 21

Consider this diem carped.
-T-shirt

Evander

I went to Kennedy's house first.

It was an hour past dawn, and the only thing in the entire house making noise was the hum of the lights as they buzzed above me.

I was staring at the note, dread making its way through my gut.

The note that said only a few words. However, those words were enough to chill me straight to the bone.

Evander,

I'm tired of being second best.

I deserve to be someone's first choice.

Thank you for giving me a few great weeks. I'll remember and cherish them for the rest of my life.

Take care of my chickens.

And that was it. Not another damn word was said. It wasn't even signed.

When I went to her closet, it was to see most of her clothes gone, some had fallen hastily to the floor. The kitchen was empty, her coffee cup still in the sink.

It was as if she'd left for a short weekend.

When I went outside, it was to find her truck still there.

I was supposed to look at it and hadn't yet.

It'd died the day prior, again, and I hadn't found time to look at it.

Her goats were gone, though, as well as her dog.

My eyes went to the chicken pen, and I realized another thing.

I didn't know how to take care of chickens.

I'd seen her do it but was that really all there was to it?

"She's gone?"

I looked behind me to see that Rafe hadn't left. He was still there, standing in the middle of the yard, waiting for me to make my decision.

Go back…or chase after Kennedy.

"She's better off without me," I said.

He snorted.

"I thought that about my sister once." Rafe looked away. "What I thought was only going to be a few months turned into years. It took me months to get back into her good graces, and even now, months later, I'm still wondering if she only tolerates me because she knows that I miss her."

I didn't know what to say to that.

He was right, though.

Kennedy may be better off without me, but at this point, I didn't think I could live without her.

She'd wormed herself into my life, planted herself so deeply into my goddamn heart that I didn't think I'd ever be man enough to let her live without me.

Why make it harder to get her back when I had the power to do it right now just by saying three words to her.

Three words that I felt. Deeply.

"Fuck," I growled. "Let's go."

Rafe waved me off. "I'll keep doing the recon."

And that was that.

He waved me off and stepped back into the shadows, disappearing into the shadows like he had never been there in the first place, leaving me free to follow after my wayward woman.

I turned away from the yard and stared blankly at the wall.

The only question was, where did she go?

***

Four hours later, I found her on a bus halfway to El Paso—the bus's destination.

The next hour was spent following behind the bus, waiting for it to stop. After sixty miles of it, I realized that it wasn't going to stop—not any time soon.

So I did what any sane man would do.

I rode my motorcycle past the bus, cut over in front of it, and started hitting my brakes.

"Here's to hoping you're paying attention, motherfucker," I growled, watching the bus in my rearview.

The bus didn't slow at first.

I assumed he thought I was taking the exit, but when I didn't, the bus started to slow.

The more I slowed, the more it slowed, until the bus driver decided to pass me.

When it went to whip over to the next lane, I followed in front of it.

This continued for another ten minutes as I pointed to the shoulder.

It was more than apparent that the bus didn't want to stop.

And I could understand that.

I was a big guy, covered in tattoos, and riding a motorcycle.

I wouldn't pull over for me either, but it was happening.

It didn't matter if I had to do this all fucking day long.

I'd do it.

Kennedy wouldn't get away from me.

It didn't get to end like that, I'd decided.

After another ten miles of this back and forth shit with the driver, the bus finally pulled over and came to a stop.

Likely, they'd called the cops, too, so I tried to make it fast.

The moment it stopped only ten feet away from me, I got off my bike and walked up to the driver's side window.

Hopefully approaching him this way wouldn't freak him out too bad.

But I could tell by the wary look in his eyes that he was freaked.

Oops.

"You have my woman on your bus, and I want to give her a ride back home," I said to the older man, likely in his early fifties.

"Why?" he asked suspiciously. "What if she doesn't want to go with you?"

I shrugged. "Why don't you ask her?"

The man pursed his lips.

"What's her name?"

I rolled my eyes.

He knew who she was. She was sitting almost directly behind him, and I saw her head poke back and forth from behind her seat for the last ten minutes.

"Kennedy."

"Kennedy who?"

I gritted my teeth. "Kennedy soon to be fuckin' Lennox."

"No, I will not!" she denied from two seats back, plastering her face against the glass window of the bus.

She was so close to the window that her nose was scrunched up, and it was causing her nostrils to open wide.

Her glare was ferocious.

I tried not to laugh.

"I can see your boogers."

She immediately removed her nose from the window, then gave me the finger.

Then, to add insult to injury, she breathed over the window, fogging it up, and wrote, 'Fuck yo'

She breathed on it again, and then wrote 'u' underneath it.

I snorted, and tried really, *really* hard not to burst out laughing like I wanted to.

Really, I did.

But the way she scrapped it once she realized how non-perfect it was, and started over, this time further from the side of the window, I just couldn't help it.

I bellowed in laughter. It couldn't be helped.

"Can't you just run him over, Mr. Bus Driver?"

I looked over to the bus driver, who was trying not to laugh right along with me.

"I can't, Ma'am," he apologized. "And since you told me I couldn't call the police, there's really nothing we can do but sit here until he moves his bike."

"You could back up?" Kennedy suggested.

The bus driver sighed. "I already thought about that, but he's got more maneuverability with that monster bike of his."

I looked over at my bike.

It wasn't really a monster. It was more of a pretty girl—at least, in my opinion.

But whatever.

"Well, that's just perfect," she snarled. "Can you open the little hatches underneath so I can get my suitcase?"

I hid my grin and winked at the bus driver, who was standing up from his seat.

"Yes, Ma'am."

I walked around the side of the bus and waited for her to get off.

The moment she did, she glared.

"How did you manage to get onto an empty bus?" I asked her, walking alongside her to the doors that were holding only a single suitcase.

"I don't want to talk to you," she snarled, turning her head away and crossing her arms over her chest while she tapped her foot impatiently.

I held my breath, then nodded my thanks to the driver when he wheeled her suitcase over to me.

"Have a good one, Ma'am," the bus driver said as he made his way back to the bus. "Don't do anything stupid, Son."

I snorted.

"Already one step ahead of you. Now I just have to get her to accept my apology."

"Like hell I'll accept anything from you," she snapped.

My eye twitched.

"Okay," I said as I rolled the bag over to my bike, then looked at the huge bag and my bike uncertainly.

I hadn't thought this part through really well.

I'd just gotten on the damn thing and took off in her direction the moment my brother confirmed that she'd been seen getting on a bus to El Paso.

Now, I was thinking that she might be mad at me when I told her that we'd have to leave some of the stuff behind.

"What do you think you're doing?" she asked as I pushed the suitcase onto its side and started unzipping it.

"We're gonna have to shove all this shit into the saddle bags," I told her. "Why do you…"

I stopped when I saw my t-shirt right on top.

She caught my raised eyebrow and narrowed her eyes.

"You can leave that one on the side of the road," she snarled.

I swear to Christ. This woman was my fuckin' heart.

"Whatever," I mumbled, setting it aside. I wouldn't be leaving it, though.

It was one of my favorite ones. I'd purchased it almost fifteen years ago when I went to see Journey in concert.

It was soft, threadbare, and fucking comfortable.

The next thing underneath my shirt was her purse, which I shoved inside the saddle bag.

The rest of her shit, which wasn't very much, went into the other bag.

The only thing that was left was a box of tampons.

"You need this now?" I asked.

She shook her head. "No."

Nodding, I tossed it back into the luggage, and then shoved the luggage further off the side of the road until it was nestled in between two trees.

"You can't just leave that here!" she cried out. "That's littering."

I raised my brows at her.

"Yeah, but I have nowhere to go with it, and we need to the get the hell off the side of the highway before we get run the fuck over."

Her eyes looked up one side of the highway and down the other.

It was long and straight, and not one single person had passed us the entire time we'd been pulled over.

"You're so full of shit," she countered. "Why are you even here?"

The venom in her voice gave me pause, then I came up like a tiger launching himself at dinner, and wrapped my arms around her before she could step away.

"I'm here because I love you," I told her. "I wanted to finish what I'd started. I wanted an ending before I gave you a beginning. I wanted to make sure that what I had to offer you wasn't tainted in that motherfucker's bullshit and lies. But you didn't wait, so I couldn't either."

Her mouth snapped shut so fast that I heard the click of her teeth.

"You're lying."

I laughed, tilting my head back and barking it at the clear blue sky.

When I finally gathered my composure, I looked back down at her, a wry smile on my face.

"How many men that don't love you would drive four hours away, breaking their parole, to bring you back?"

She sniffed at me.

"I don't really care."

"You don't care if I go back to jail?" I asked.

She nodded, looking away.

"Then why didn't you let the driver call the cops when I was trying to get y'all to pull over?" I teased.

She shrugged.

"That was his idea," she lied.

Bringing my hand up to her face, I cupped it and tilted her chin, forcing her to look at me.

She gave me her best scowl.

"All that face makes me want to do is kiss it," I informed her.

She glared even harder, narrowing her eyes to mere slits.

"I don't care what you want," she hissed. "Let me go."

I did and she stepped away.

"What now?" I questioned.

"Now you take me to where I wanted to go."

I sighed.

"What's in it for me?"

"What do you mean what's in it for you?" she growled.

It was so cute I wanted to pinch her little cheeks.

"I mean, what's in it for me?" I asked. "If I take you to El Paso, what is that going to accomplish?"

"It's going to accomplish me going to where I want to go," she said, sounding confused. "What else would it accomplish?"

I decided that maybe she needed to be fucked into a better mood, so I did just that.

I stalked toward her, and pulled her into my arms, even though she tried to step back once again.

"Let me go!" she shrieked.

"No."

Then I slammed my mouth down onto hers.

She bit my tongue and I pulled back with a growl.

"You want to play rough?" I checked to make sure.

Because if I did this, it wasn't going to be nice. If she fought me, I wouldn't be able to help myself.

I knew she wanted it.

I could see the way her nipples were pebbled, and the fact that the only thing she was doing was being mean, which was enough to cement the fact that she wanted me.

Her breathing was choppy, and her neck was flushed red.

Her eyes were soft and heavy, like she wanted me just as bad as I wanted her.

"You're going to get on that bike, and you're going to take me to El Paso," she ordered, pointing her finger at me.

I laughed at her, and then caught her wrist, spinning her around, forcing her up against my body.

"I'm not taking you anywhere but my home, where you'll be moving in with me," I informed her. "And then you're going to put my ring on your finger, and we're going to get married at the county courthouse tomorrow."

She struggled to free herself.

"Macho asshole doesn't suit you," she grunted, pushing both elbows back at once.

I shifted, then dropped my mouth to her neck, causing her to cease all movement.

The moment my beard met her skin, I opened my mouth and ran the tip of my tongue along the cords of her neck.

"Spent every fucking second, of every fucking day since I've met you, thinking about you. Worrying about you. Wondering if you've eaten yet," I whispered against her skin. "I've slept with you only a handful of times, but it was enough to know that I don't ever want to sleep without you again."

A sob caught in her throat, and she dropped her head, her hands clutching mine where they were wrapped around her waist.

"I didn't say I love you, but that doesn't mean that I didn't fucking feel it." I bit down lightly on her shoulder, then soothed the hurt with my tongue. "Say it again."

She shook her head. The soft tendrils of her hair got stuck in my beard, but I didn't care.

Nothing was more important than saying the words back to her.

I just had to get her to repeat hers, first.

Still, she didn't say them.

Time to pull out the big guns.

Ripping my chest open to reveal my heart was hard. Every time I opened myself up to someone, they did nothing but disappoint me.

It fucking hurt when people didn't reciprocate, but the thing with Kennedy? Yeah, it wasn't fake. It wasn't something that could even be quantified.

It was real.

She was real.

And I needed her to know that I was in this one hundred percent.

"I want to have babies with you."

Her legs started to tremble.

"All those times that we didn't use a condom?"

She shivered.

"I want you to get knocked up."

She inhaled shakily.

"I want to see you pregnant with my child. I want to see you around town with everyone knowing that I put him inside of you."

I tilted her head back by latching onto her hair.

Her eyes were filled with tears; one spilled over.

I kissed it away.

"I love you, woman. Lock, stock, and barrel. Down to my bones. Everything that I have to give is yours. It may not be much, but it's all that I have to give, and I want you to have it."

She closed her eyes, and she lost the battle with her tears.

They spilled over.

At first, I tried to stem the flow, but soon I realized how futile an effort that was, and decided that maybe hugging her would be best.

So that's what I did.

I held her while she cried in my arms on the side of a deserted Texas highway.

Her crying put me into a weird mood.

One where I was starting to get pissed at myself for causing all of this heartache for her.

In fact, I was so lost in thought, berating myself for doing stupid shit all the time, that I didn't watch what was happening right in front of me.

Sure, I was looking at her—or more honestly, the top of her head—but I wasn't paying attention to the fact that she was no longer crying.

Nor was I paying attention to her hands.

Not until they were on the zipper of my jeans.

"What are you doing?" I questioned her, stepping back slightly.

The move gave her more room to do what she wanted, which was unzip my pants.

"I'm touching you inappropriately," she said. "Right here in public."

I thought she was joking, and I was about to tease her, but then she dipped her small hand into the gap of my jeans, cupping my half-hard cock in her hand.

A half-hard cock that only stayed half hard for all of three seconds before it filled with blood.

Which was about the time she tried to pull it out of the small opening in my jeans.

I winced and pulled away.

Her hand stayed in my pants, though, and she glared.

"What?" she asked. "You're saying I can't do this?"

I grinned, and then circled her wrist with my hand.

"No," I said. "I'm saying that my dick literally will not fit through that opening. I know from experience."

She blinked.

"If you want to do something, like suck my cock, you're going to have to open my belt first."

Her eyes turned calculating.

"You'd want that?"

I stared at her blankly.

"I'd want what?" I questioned. "My dick sucked by my woman?"

She nodded.

"What kind of question is that?" I teased, pulling her in by a hand hooked around her neck. "Let me tell you something, honey. If you offered to suck my cock in the middle of a crowded restaurant, I'd probably let you do it. I don't think a man alive has ever said no to a blow job by an attractive woman."

She giggled, then dropped to her knees.

My mouth fell slightly open.

"You're going to hurt your knees…" my voice trailed off when she yanked open my belt and yanked hard on the button of my jeans.

"You think we should at least move further off the road?" I wondered gruffly.

She pulled the front of my jeans down slowly, and then moaned when she got the first good look at my cock's base.

In fact, she was so enraptured with the first sight of it, she forgot what she was doing, and leaned forward to lick the base while the waistband of my underwear cut off circulation to the rest of my cock.

But the moment she pressed that hot tongue to the base and trailed up the vein to where my cock was being bisected by my underwear, I threw my head back and moaned.

"Fucking goddammit," I found myself saying.

I hadn't been aware that the base of my cock was even all that sensitive; but apparently, it was.

Greatly so.

"I wonder if I could take all of you up to right here," she blew a breath along the line where her tongue had traced along my bare skin. "It'd take a lot of practice."

I couldn't stand it anymore and reached forward, putting the palm of my hand over her ear.

"Seriously should go back into the shadows at least," I muttered, gritting my teeth lightly when she reached forward and tugged down the front of my boxer briefs.

My cock bounced free, bobbing lightly with the beat of my heart.

She reached forward and encircled the middle of my cock with her hand and gave it a few expert pumps.

I closed my eyes in bliss.

Then I felt the heat of her mouth on my tip right before she circled her tongue around it like one would a melting ice cream cone as they tried to catch all the drips at once.

I saw stars.

With her down on the ground, knees likely uncomfortable as hell due to the uneven road, I could do nothing but watch. It was hard to convince her why we shouldn't be doing this, especially with her choking on my cock.

Literally choking. Each time she would push forward, I would hit the back of her throat, and she'd try to push a little bit past where she'd gone the first time.

Then she swallowed, and all of those beautiful muscles in her throat clamped down on my cock tightly, stealing my breath.

"Fuck!" I grunted, circling the base of my cock with my own fist, halting my release that was already boiling in my balls.

"Get up," I barked.

She pulled off my cock and stood, looking at me uneasily.

"Bend over the back of the bike."

She blinked at me.

"Now!"

I started to slowly work my fist up the length of my shaft, waiting for her to comply.

Which she did.

Only, before I could do anything crazy like rip her jeans down to her ankles and plunge inside of her, I heard the unmistakable sound of a motor.

"Fuck," I grunted, going up to her and pulling her up and spinning her around.

I pinned my cock between us, holding her close, and waited for the car to pass.

It did moments later, topping the hill from the opposite direction in which we'd been headed earlier, and passing us all within five seconds.

Only, they pulled over about a hundred yards down from us.

"Goddammit," I grumbled.

I looked down at the woman in my arms.

"This is all your fault," I grunted, pulling her into my hold tighter than before.

She blinked her eyes at me innocently.

"What did I do?"

I leaned down and nipped the side of her neck with my teeth, causing her to jerk in surprise.

My cock twitched between us.

She batted her eyelids.

"Y'all okay?"

I looked up at the shout, and saw a man half leaning out of the window of his truck, staring at me like I was crazy.

Sure, my bike was kind of hanging out in the road, but I suppose it wasn't every day that you saw a couple kissing on the side of the highway…even if we were in the middle of Podunk, Texas.

"I'm fine, thank you. Just stopped to stretch our legs."

My words turned from sure and confident, to a high-pitched squeak at the end due to Kennedy raising her hand and encircling it around the head of my cock.

When she swiped her thumb over the hole and collected the fluid that'd started to form there, my eyes nearly crossed.

I cleared my throat. "Thank you for asking, though."

The man waved and then took off without another word.

I stayed where I was, glaring down at the woman in my arms who didn't even have the decency to look up at me, until the man was so far away that I could barely see him any longer.

"That was fucking rude," I growled, then lifted her up into my arms and started walking into the trees off the side of the road.

She easily circled my hips with her legs, and locked them behind her back. Though, as we walked, she started to unbutton her jeans.

When she shoved her hands down the front of her pants, and came back out with wet fingers, I leaned forward and sucked them clean.

"Fuck me," she whispered.

I couldn't tell if it was a demand or an exclamation. Whatever it was, I chose to take it as an invitation and dropped her down into the pine needles as far into the trees as I could in my presently over-excited condition.

I could see the road where I was at, and my bike, which meant if anyone looked hard enough, they could likely see us, too.

But at this point, with a hard, throbbing, still-wet-from-her-mouth cock, the taste of her on my tongue and the feel of her in my arms, I no longer had the control, or the will, to care.

With swift movements, I yanked both her panties and jeans down the length of her legs, and then used the bunched fabric as a handhold to roll her over to her belly.

She whipped over so fast that I had to hold in a laugh at the look of surprise on her face.

"Holy shit!" she cried out. "That was like, super-fast!"

I grunted and started to work my cock again.

"Up on your knees," I ordered her. "This has to be fast and hard, because my bike's hanging on to the road, and if anybody looks hard enough, they'll know exactly what we're doing out here."

She got up on her knees and looked at me over her shoulder.

"Do you care?"

I grinned and lined my cock up with her entrance, moaning into my throat at the feel of her heat against the head of my cock.

"If I get caught and go back to jail, that means I won't have this to come home to every night," I informed her. "So yes, I care."

Then I thrust forward, so hard and suddenly, that she squeaked in surprise.

I only got my cock halfway in before I had to pull back out, but the next thrust had my cock sinking all the way home.

No extra inches left out.

She'd taken every single inch I had to give.

"Fuck, fuck, fuck," she whimpered.

I squeezed my eyes tightly shut and counted to ten as I tried to get myself under control.

"Are you okay?" I growled low in my throat.

Her pussy muscles were clenching around me spasmodically, and I was finding it hard to draw breath into my lungs.

"Yesssss," she drew out the 's' like a snake. "Pleasssssse."

I pulled back and then thrust forward again.

But this time, she met me with a push of her own, causing me to thrust into her so roughly that I was scared that I'd hurt her.

She easily shot that worry out of the air, though, when she leaned forward, pulling her body away from my cock, and then slamming herself backwards on to it again.

She did this, over and over again, and I did nothing but watch her fuck herself with my cock.

I leaned back, entranced with the play of muscles around her ass, and the way her butt cheeks jiggled.

"I love your ass," I told her, running one finger down the part, circling that forbidden entrance.

She mewled something when my thumb passed over it a second time.

I grinned.

"You ever had anybody in your ass, baby?" I knew the answer to that seeing as she had been a virgin.

She shook her head.

"You want me in your ass?"

Her wide, startled eyes looked at me over her shoulder, and then she started moving again.

"Yes."

One word, but it was enough for my hand to clamp down onto her ass as need shot through my body.

How would she feel around my cock?

Certainly, she'd strangle me.

I was big. *Really* big.

It'd probably hurt her the first time, but not too bad.

Not if I went slow and lubed her up.

Fuck, just the thought of taking her there was enough to send tiny shocks of need shooting down into my balls.

And then she stopped.

The tiny shocks went away, and I opened my eyes to see her staring at me.

"Are you going to participate?"

I grinned.

Then I started to participate.

Lani Lynn Vale

CHAPTER 22

Na^16
-Batman

Kennedy

We got back to Hostel in five hours.

Evander had stopped to feed me after two, and then we'd gotten back on the road again.

The ride was pure torture.

My knees were bruised. My vagina was sore, and each and every bump along the way reminded me of the roughness I experienced at the deft hands of the man that had declared me as his.

And I'd loved every single second of it.

I was exhausted by the time I got home, and nearly lost it when I saw my dog and my goats back where they belonged.

The only thing that held those tears in check was Evander's arm around my shoulders, guiding me into the house and to my bedroom.

"How'd you know?"

I expected him to find out that I was gone well after I arrived at my destination—which hadn't really been much of a destination, if I was being honest.

When he'd left, his eyes set on revenge, I'd decided that I needed to leave, too. So I went.

Second best sucked.

Second best was what I always seemed to be, yet never wanted to experience.

When had I started settling?

I shouldn't have to settle…not with the man that I loved.

I'd walked into town, which had been interesting seeing as I'd had three goats and a dog with me the whole way. The first car I'd seen had been Evander's brother, so I'd tied the goats and the dog up to the Jeep's door handle, and I'd left him a note.

The entire fifteen-minute walk to the bus station, I'd cried.

Which had gotten me on the bus that was leaving to go pick up a set of passengers in El Paso.

The bus driver had been very nice and understanding, and he agreed to take me despite the fact that it'd been against company policy.

Though, I couldn't tell if he gave in due to the tears that were still in my eyes, or the fact that I practically begged him to take me.

Either way, I'd gone, and had been out of town with just a freakin' carry-on sized bag in tow, all within about an hour of Evander leaving.

The whole time, I'd refused to think about how that made me feel to have him leave without saying a word to me.

I'd told him I loved him, for God's sake, and he'd just looked at me.

Looked at me.

His eyes hadn't flared. His hand didn't shoot out and wrap around my neck like he did when I'd said something he liked.

Hell, he hadn't even blinked.

He'd just left.

That'd been it.

No dramatics. No overheated, angry words were exchanged.

One second he was standing in front of me, and the next he'd been walking down the sidewalk.

Then he'd stopped and my heart had swelled.

Only, when he'd turned around, it was to call out to his freakin' dog.

Not that that dog wasn't awesome…but it was his dog, goddammit.

And that'd been the straw that broke the camel's back, so to speak.

"What are you talking about…" I started to ask.

I tripped over something on the floor and went down hard.

My arms went out in front of me, and I fell…right next to a dead, decapitated chicken.

My face exploded in pain.

My stomach started to lurch, but I held it in check…just barely.

I was much calmer than I was the first time.

I stood up, or rather, I was hauled up by the waist by two big hands, and stared at the carnage before me.

"Oh, God."

Oh, God. Oh, God. Oh, God.

They were all dead.

Again.

Every last one of them.

Twenty-nine chickens.

Little Ethel that I'd gotten from the feed store was among them with her missing back right toe.

Martha Stewart, the Ameraucana with the crooked beak.

Donna, my Easter Egger with the twisted foot. It didn't take me long to love my new flock. I'd already named them all. They were mine. All twenty-three of the new flock and my six chicks were dead.

The cursing followed, and I was turned in big, strong arms.

My face was pressed into a hard chest.

I was in shock.

The chest I was pressed against rumbled, but I didn't hear what it was saying.

Dead.

Dead.

Dead.

"No," I whispered brokenly. "No, no, no."

Something slippery was on my hands, and I felt something hot on my face.

No, no, no, no.

I chanted it like it was my lifeline, thinking about how I'd just left only five hours ago.

All that damage had been done while I was supposed to be at home.

They'd been locked up in a fenced-in coop, for God's sake!

"Bro, need you to come over here."

Seven words that were enough to partially pierce through my shock.

Evander didn't talk to his brother. Not willingly, anyway.

"Yeah, I'm at home. Or Kennedy's house."

I looked up and found Evander looking down at me, then he started to curse.

"Fuck me."

Exactly nine minutes later, I was at the clinic in town, being seen by a very, very, very pregnant woman.

"What happened?" the woman asked.

Her nametag read: Hannah, R.N.

She moved, and the bulge of her belly brushed against my arm.

Her hand went to my forehead, and she lightly brushed my hair away from what I now realized was a large gash right above my eyebrow.

I was holding my wrist protectively against my belly, and I was sure I looked a sight.

Chicken blood, my blood, and a mixture of dirt and gravel stained my clothes.

Before I could answer, a knock sounded at the door.

"Hannah?"

I turned to find the doctor standing in the room, his eyes not on me or Hannah, but on Evander.

"Yeah?" Hannah asked distractedly.

"There's a very anxious man in the waiting room saying that you aren't supposed to be here. Something about how you're pregnant and overdue, and you keep having false labor. He wants to be there if anything happens. False or not."

She sighed and turned.

"I'm about to help you stitch this up, and then I'm headed out to go get my daughter from my brother's house. Tell him that I'll talk to him later and if the status of my pregnancy changes, he'll be the first one to know."

The doctor still wasn't looking at her.

He was staring at Evander with a hard look, his eyes jumping from him to the gash on my forehead, then to Evander again.

I knew what he was thinking. He thought that Evander had done this.

I saw the moment that he decided to question him, too.

"Are you okay in here with him?"

That question was directed at Evander.

"Yeah," Hannah said distractedly. Her attention was again on my head. "You can send Dr. Montgomery in, though."

The doctor hesitated.

Evander grunted something.

"I'm going to go outside. My brother is here and I want to tell him what's going on anyway. If you need me, yell out, and I'll come."

Evander said this while looking at me like I might lose it, and to some extent, he was right to do so.

I *was* about to lose it.

But with this doctor giving Evander the stink eye, I was better able to control myself—or, at least, my tears.

I was a doomed crazy chicken lady.

Maybe I just needed to find a job somewhere.

"You okay?"

I looked up at the pregnant chick that was still touching me.

"Yeah," I muttered. "Do you know anywhere that's hiring?"

Her eyes flicked down to me, and I was struck with shock.

Despite her huge, obviously pregnant state, she was freakin' beautiful.

"You in trouble?"

I shook my head, and then thought better of it and nodded.

"Yes and no."

"Have anything to do with this cut on your face?"

I shook my head.

"No."

"Huh," she muttered. "Could've fooled me."

I sighed.

"It has nothing to do with Evander," I told her. "That's the man I'm going to marry someday."

Her mouth quirked.

"Someday?"

I nodded.

"Yeah, someday," I sighed.

"I have a someday, too," she admitted. "He's the one the doctor was just talking about."

"Ahh," I sighed. "That's an alpha male thing, I suppose. I tried to leave. Was halfway to El Paso when he came riding up on his Harley and told me to get off the bus."

She snickered.

"I thought I went into labor yesterday."

My eyes widened.

"Are you Travis' Hannah?" I asked. "I was there when he got the call. He freaked way out, and his eyes went all saucer like, and I swear to God, I thought he was going to pass out."

Her smile was sad.

"Yeah, that's what I keep getting from him, too."

I snickered as she cleaned the blood from my face and winced slightly when she hit a sore spot.

"Was he like that with y'all's first one?" I asked her.

She smiled warmly.

"Travis isn't the father of my first daughter. Only this one," she gestured down to her stomach with a tilt of her head.

My brows furrowed.

"But they said he had another kid…"

Hannah's face twisted.

"He does…one who he only ever sees on holidays. One who hates his guts. One who is behind the reason why he wants nothing to do with me or the one he's about to have."

I watched her face closely, and then decided that I wasn't going to make her keep talking about this subject since it was obviously bothering her.

She moved again, and her stomach brushed my arm, and I felt the distinct thump of something kicking me, almost as if he was pissed off that I'd intruded on his space.

"Your baby just kicked me," I informed her, even though she could more than likely feel it on her end.

Though, she'd have to be freakin' paralyzed not to feel the force from that kick.

She grinned. "A booger like his daddy."

She hummed something else I couldn't quite catch under her breath and brought up a piece of gauze off the tray next to the bed.

"I want you to hold this here while I go get the doctor to stitch this up." She gestured with her hand. "I'll be right..."

A commotion from out in the other room had me standing up and heading to the door.

Hannah had been on her way, too, but she was much slower than I was, despite my injuries.

I opened the door just in time to see two men—two police officers—throw Evander to the floor.

He hit so roughly that his face bounced off the tile floor.

"What are you doing?" I shrieked, running into the fray.

That's when a hand planted in my chest, and I fell backwards, hitting the floor on my ass.

Hard.

Evander hadn't been struggling before.

But seeing a man put his hands on me, he went fucking wild.

"I'm okay!" I started to crawl to him. "I'm okay!"

I'd just gotten a hand on his head when a rough hand latched onto my arm and pulled me away.

"Go sit the fuck down, or better yet, go back to the room you were just in. I'll come for your statement later."

"What statement?" I demanded, kicking as I was dragged across the room on my ass.

"Hey!" Hannah called out. "Let her go! Can't you see that she's hurt?"

The man who had his hand latched onto my arm let me go, and he rounded on her.

"How about y'all go back in there, and don't worry about what's going on out here?"

"I'll worry about it if I want to worry about it, motherfucker!"

We all froze at those words coming out of a very pregnant, beautiful woman's mouth.

But not for long.

The cop rounded on Hannah, ready to push her, but, suddenly, Travis was there, stopping him before he could even take a step

"Officer Rogers," Travis' voice was low and barely controlled. "I seriously suggest that you rethink what you're about to do, because I'm not above beating the shit out of you in front of witnesses."

I finally looked at the officer that had yanked me around like a rag doll.

Officer Rogers. The cop who had asked me out and I turned down. The one whose truck I had helped Evander to recover.

Holy *shit*.

More struggling from the other side of Officer Rogers had me turning to see Evander still struggling on the floor.

"Let him go!" I screamed, my fingernails digging into my palms.

That's when I saw Evander's brother was one of the arresting officers that had thrown him to the ground and allowed his poor face to hit the floor.

"Walter," I whispered. "What are you doing?"

The accusation in my voice was enough to make Walter wince.

Evander's eyes looked fucking ravaged.

"Don't, baby," he insisted gently. "Just don't."

My throat felt tight, and I couldn't get my legs to work.

I wanted to go to him. I wanted to pull him into my arms.

I started to crawl.

"Travis," Evander barked as he was yanked to his feet.

Travis' angry eyes came down to me, but I didn't stop despite Travis' attempt at reaching for me.

No, I crawled across the floor, past the asshole, Officer Rogers, straight to Evander, coming up to my feet about halfway and throwing myself at him.

I hit him hard and wrapped both of my arms around his neck.

His hands were restrained behind his back with cuffs, so he could do nothing but drop his head to my shoulder and kiss my neck.

"Don't do this," he whispered to me. "Be good. Don't do this."

Then he was yanked away from me, causing me to stumble.

His eyes met mine once more, and then he was gone, being led out of the small clinic with Officer Rogers the asshole following right behind him, shooting daggers at Travis and me as he went.

I watched as Walter opened the back door of the cruiser, and then moved out of the way for the other officer to shove Evander—none too gently—into the back before slamming the door.

Words were discussed among the officers, and it was then that I saw Evander's parole officer out there as well.

My heart started to beat double time.

"What's going on, Travis?"

That was my nurse, Hannah.

I didn't bother to turn around, instead watching as the cruiser pulled away, leaving Evander's brother the only one left on the scene.

And suddenly I found myself irrational.

I pushed the door open and stomped down the walkway, straight up to the awful man.

"You're a despicable, disgusting excuse for a human being," I told him. "I can't believe I ever left my goats to you. You'd probably eat them."

Walter flinched at my words.

"I had to."

My brows rose.

"You had to?" I laughed humorlessly, and it hurt my own ears to hear. "You also had a responsibility to your own brother," I snapped. "Or is that how you treat family around here?"

Walter's face shut down completely.

"I can't protect him when he's stupid," he hissed. "And I'm not sure what it is that you wanted me to do? I didn't tell him to commit any crimes."

My mouth dropped open.

"You don't truly believe that your brother would do anything like that, do you?" I asked. "Because if you do, you're fucking stupid."

Walter's jaw muscles worked as he clenched his jaw.

"There's stuff you don't know."

I stared at him like the little worm that he was.

"There's stuff *you* don't know," I told him. "Like the fact that your brother is the most beautiful, caring, loving, helpful person in the whole goddamn world."

"He committed a crime," Walter snapped.

"You believe that about as much as I believe you actually care about him," Travis countered from behind me.

It was good to know that I wasn't the only one that was disappointed in Walter.

"I'm not a detective," Walter shot back. "I'm a fucking police officer. I have to do what I'm told, or I lose my job."

"What's the point of having the job if the people you work for are shit-ass dirty?"

That was me, eloquent as always.

His eyes sliced from Travis to me.

"Someone has to make a difference."

I started to laugh.

"Oh, that's fucking rich, coming from you. Someone has to make a difference?" I brought my hand up to my face and swiped at the tears leaking from my eyes. "You're not the one making a difference, you fool—Evander is! You're just another one of the spineless, pieces of shit with a badge who don't do anything other than toe the dirty cop line in this town."

With that, I started stomping toward the truck, thankful that I'd seen where Evander kept his spare key.

Poor Gertie looked fit to be tied, and as I opened the door, I could tell he was just as unhappy about seeing his master carried away in cuffs as I was.

"Let's go, Gert," I called to the dog. "We're going to the police station."

"Wait."

I got into the truck and turned to see Travis there, staring at me.

Hannah was just behind him, holding onto his waistband, her face pale.

"What?"

I was tired.

I wanted this God-awful night to be over. I wanted to go home and sleep in my own bed, wrapped up in Evander's arms.

Not that that would be happening any time soon, but that's where my thoughts were.

"I'm calling the boys," he said. "And I have a few favors I can call in…it's gonna hurt like a bitch, but I can't see Evander go through this again."

Relief poured through me.

"What should I do?"

Should I wait? Go to the station? Call a lawyer?

I didn't know what to do. I'd never had to bail someone out of jail before.

"Go to the club," he ordered. "I'll call the boys and pull them in from their jobs. Atticus will let you in. I'm going to take her home…"

262

"You will not. I'm going with you," Hannah argued.

Travis turned to disagree, but she held up her hand.

"I'll catch a ride with her once I get the doctor to stitch her up."

Travis' jaw clenched, but he turned and looked at me.

It was then that the trickle of blood ran down my face reminded me that I had a gaping wound in my forehead.

"Oh yeah," I said. "I forgot."

In all the excitement, I'd definitely had my mind elsewhere.

"All right," Travis sighed. "Keep Gertie with you, though. Yeah?"

I looked over at Gertie, and then nodded my head. "Yeah."

CHAPTER 23

I would be the first person to die in a horror movie. I refuse to spend my last few minutes running.
-Kennedy's secret thoughts

Kennedy

An hour and four minutes later, I was walking into the club with Hannah at my side.

Atticus let us in, just as Travis had said he would, and we were now walking in the direction of the raised voices.

I looked over at Hannah, my eyes wide, and stopped just outside of the door.

Listening.

See, here is the thing about alpha men.

They thought that women were incapable of hearing and dealing with the hard stuff.

Sure, there were times that we couldn't…but this wasn't one of them.

They thought to protect us by keeping things from us—big things. Things that I would never keep away from them had the situation been reversed.

So to make sure that I didn't miss anything, I stopped and listened to the men talking, just to make sure I got all the information.

"Called in a few markers."

I didn't recognize the voice.

"Know a cop out of Louisiana, and his club president is some fucking mastermind when it comes to getting information," the voice said. "He's going to call his president and get back to me."

"I called in a few favors, too," another voice, this one somewhat familiar, agreed. "He's fucking amazing with computers. He's going to do some digging in the PD's files, see what he turns up."

Rafe. The man that'd been with Evander—his friend that was in town to help him.

"I called my ex brother-in-law," Travis said. "He's actually not too far away, so he's going to drop by. He's a Texas Ranger...he has no problem doing some investigations into the bullshit swirling around this goddamn town."

"Should've called him a long time ago, to be honest."

One of Travis' brothers, but I couldn't tell which one.

"What are we going to do about his woman?" the man I didn't know asked. "She's not going to sit tight and let him sit in jail."

I chose that moment to edge around the corner and cross my arms over my chest.

"You're right," I said evenly. "I won't."

My eyes roamed around the room, and I took in each man, making sure to make eye contact, and then turned to Travis. "What was their reason for arresting him?"

I knew that he hadn't been caught going out of town. Something like that wouldn't have warranted the reaction that it did.

"Woman vet across the road is dead, and Evander's prints were found on a gate at the scene."

I blinked.

"You're full of fucking shit," I said. "Evander wasn't at the scene. I was with him for the last five hours."

"Where?" Walter snapped.

I'd seen him, of course, but I hadn't acknowledged him. Piece of shit wasn't getting anything from me. I'd rather talk to the devil himself than him.

I couldn't tell him where, exactly, because then that'd be putting Evander in violation of his parole. But he hadn't been doing anything wrong. I knew that, so I did what I had to do.

"Where, honey?" Travis asked softly. "This would be best if you gave us all the information you had."

My eyes turned to the dark, dangerous looking man in the corner. The one who had come here to help Evander with his revenge.

He knew where I'd been, yet he wasn't saying anything either.

"He was with me, on his bike…doing stuff," I said, a blush suffusing my face. "I was upset, and he and I were talking."

Travis grunted something and Walter growled.

"Where were you?" he asked. "It's not going to be enough if you don't have some sort of proof that he was with you."

I turned to Travis.

"What's the time frame?" I asked, digging through my purse. "We stopped two towns over and got some food. I have the receipt right here."

Thank God we'd stopped closer to home.

"About two hours ago."

"There's still a possibility that he could've made it home," Walter snapped. "That's not good enough."

I gritted my teeth. "Well, when I got home, my chickens had all been slaughtered, which you already know. We took about twenty minutes cleaning that up and ensuring that none of them were suffering before we went to the clinic, where we sat for another half an hour waiting to be seen. That's about four hours right there that he has an alibi for, and the night before that, I was with him sleeping in our bed."

Walter growled. "I'm not trying to be an asshole here, Kennedy. I'm trying to tell you that it's not going to be good enough. Not with his prints found at the scene."

"Circumstantial," I said.

I'd watched enough CSI to know that finding prints at the scene was nothing like finding a murder weapon in Evander's car.

"How was the woman done?"

That came from the man I'd never seen before.

"Who are you and why are you here?" Walter mumbled, looking away.

"I'm Brock," Brock announced. "And I work here. Why are you here?"

Walter looked at me. "She said I didn't care about him. I'm here to prove that I do. I'm supposed to be at work right now. Instead I'm here, trying to fucking help."

I narrowed my eyes at him.

"Your chance to help was a long time ago."

"Kennedy," Travis sighed, pinching the bridge of his nose. "Not helping."

I shut my mouth.

He was right. It wasn't.

But I couldn't help myself.

I took a seat, though, and crossed my arms over my chest.

"You wanna know what I think?"

That was Rafe.

"What?" Travis groaned.

"I think that the chief is corrupt. I also think that shit's going down in this place that y'all have no fucking clue about."

Rafe's words, although impassive, were unnervingly correct.

"That officer hurt me, and he didn't need to," I agreed, lifting the sleeve of my t-shirt up and showing the room at large. "Evander's going to lose his mind when he sees this."

Breaths were drawn as they saw the bruises.

They looked pretty gnarly, that was for sure. Dark black and purple splotches in the shape of a handprint about the size of one particular police officer's hand.

"What I think is that Balthazar has people in this town in his pocket."

My brow lifted in surprise.

I hadn't actually witnessed anything first hand, but I'd heard about him through Evander. I knew that he was targeted by this man. I knew that, more than likely, this Balthazar character had dirt on everyone and was either blackmailing those people into helping him or those individuals were just as dirty as him.

If that were the case, then I was a little confused and a whole lot more suspicious as to why Walter was even here.

It was more than obvious that there was no love lost between these two brothers, but maybe there was still some loyalty towards each other left. Walter had to feel something for his brother, even if it was just mutual respect.

Rafe's words about the town being in Balthazar's pocket weren't all that surprising considering the way things happened here.

And suddenly I was mad all over again.

Crossing my arms over my chest, I squared my shoulders and sent a rather impressive—at least I thought so—glare toward Walter.

"Can't you do anything?"

My words were simple, but the meaning behind them couldn't be denied...not by anyone in the room.

I'd pretty much implied that Walter was no good here if he wasn't going to do anything about his brother being in jail.

Walter opened his mouth to reply when someone's phone rang.

I looked in the direction it'd come from, and stared as the new guy, Brock, lifted the phone to his ear and said, "Yeah?"

I studied his features.

He was quite eye catching.

He had dark brown hair that had hints of red in it when he turned just right and the light caught it. His eyes were a muddy brown that, at first glance, weren't all that impressive.

What was impressive, however, was watching that color change before my eyes.

So not brown eyes, but actually hazel.

He was strongly built with large, muscular arms. His shoulders were wide, and from what I could see of his waist that was above the table, it was trim and taut.

He was wearing a black, long-sleeved shirt and dirty blue jeans.

His hands had black staining on them, likely meaning that he'd come straight from work and hadn't even had a chance to wash his hands yet.

For some reason, knowing that he hadn't even taken the time to wash up caused my eyes to fill.

I dashed my hand under my eyes, and I looked away, only to spot Hannah looking at me. Looking was too vague, actually. She was watching me so intently, it was like she was trying to bore a hole into my face with her eyes.

"What?" I whispered.

"I think you should file a complaint, too." She nodded toward her arm. "I'll do the same. He intimidated me. My brother's actually been texting me. He's not happy."

"Fuck."

I looked over to see Travis run his hand through his hair.

"What?"

"Michael and Travis don't get along," Hannah explained. "In fact, that's too tame of a description for the animosity that they have for each other."

I sensed a story, and if this were any other situation, I'd demand to know more.

But this wasn't a normal situation. This was a fucking tragedy and I was literally at my breaking point.

Any more information at this point might very well kill me.

I nodded but looked away.

I didn't know what to do.

Didn't know what to say.

The only thing I knew was that I wanted to go down to that police station and file a report…which is exactly what I was going to fucking do.

Right the fuck now.

I turned around and left, my feet taking me to Evander's truck before I even knew where I was going.

Time for operation: Get Evander Out of Jail So He Didn't Kill Anybody.

***

I stomped up the front walk of the police station and went straight to the first person I saw, which was a woman behind a glass partition.

She looked startled to find me in front of her as fast as I was walking and smiled a little nervously at me.

"How may I help you?" she questioned, crossing her hands over the desk calendar in front of her.

"I'm here to file a complaint against a police officer," I told her. "Who would I do that with?"

She looked around nervously.

Maybe she was new?

"I…" she hesitated. "Hold on one moment."

She got up and scurried away.

"You've scared the poor girl."

I looked up at mystery man, also known as Rafe, and shrugged.

"I don't care."

"Huh," he grunted. "What are you going to do?"

I clenched my hands in front of me, and stared at the glass like it'd done me a grievous wrong.

"I'm going to file a complaint against Officer Rogers, and then I'm going to demand they let me see Evander to make sure that he's all right," I told him honestly.

Rafe snorted.

"They won't let you see him to make sure that he's all right," Rafe replied. "But they'll take your complaint."

He pulled out his phone and dialed a number, said a few words, and then hung up.

I lifted my brows at him, and he shrugged.

Obviously, he wasn't going to tell me. Whatever.

I waited for a few more minutes for someone to come back to the window before I finally had enough.

Pulling out my own phone this time, I dialed 911.

Rafe didn't say a word, though I knew he'd seen the numbers.

"9-1-1, what's your emergency?"

I gritted my teeth.

"A police officer hurt me. I'm standing in the police station but nobody is coming to help me."

"Ma'am…"

I knew what she was going to say. This wasn't an emergency.

Well, I really didn't give a fuck. Not at this point.

"I'll need you to find someone to get out here and take my statement, or I'll be calling the local news station as well as the newspaper next. If that doesn't work, I'll start calling national news stations," I snapped.

Then I hung up.

I only waited two minutes before the doors on the side of the room opened up, and a haggard looking police officer came out, his eyes weary.

I smiled at him and that seemed to make him even more wary.

"Ma'am." He offered me his hand. "How may I help you?"

I grinned. "You can take my statement."

CHAPTER 24

Eat the tacos, your cowboy boots will still fit.
-Fact of life

Evander

I was released within four hours of my arrest, and I had an idea that had a lot to do with the fact that my woman had come to the police station and pleaded my case.

"Don't leave town, Lennox."

I flipped the officer off, Detective Mueller, the same one who'd done a shitty job investigating my case the first time around, and kept walking.

"Watch your step, boy."

I halted and turned, causing Detective Mueller to reach for his service weapon.

But that was all I did. I only watched him watch me, but it was enough.

He wouldn't be saying anymore stupid bullshit…at least not to my face.

"Have a good night, Mueller."

Then I walked out, unsurprised to find Kennedy there, already waiting for me.

The moment the door shut, she was sprinting toward me.

Her face looked like shit, and she already had the start of a black eye forming.

I stopped just short of her and braced myself by dropping one foot back.

Thank God.

The moment she was close enough, she launched herself at me, practically strangling me with her arms.

I coughed slightly and held her just a little bit tighter, then remembered the whispered words between the two officers from earlier, right outside my cell.

"Let me see your arm," I demanded, setting her away from me.

Resigned that I wouldn't stop until I saw the state of her arm, she took one more step back and lifted the sleeve of her shirt up to her shoulder.

What I saw made my eyes go wide.

"Holy shit." I delicately allowed my fingers to move down her arm, just barely brushing her skin.

The move was enough to cause her to flinch, though.

"I'm going to fuckin' kill him," I turned on my heel and started my stomp back inside.

She halted me by fitting her hand into the gap between my back and my waistband.

"Don't," she ordered. "I'm starving. Take me for food and then we'll go back to the club and discuss what's to be done next."

I stopped, but only because I knew she wouldn't let go. She'd let me drag her inside with me before she did.

I clenched my fists at my waist and dropped my head, counting to ten very slowly.

When I got there, I decided that ten wasn't long enough to get this kind of anger under control and continued on to twenty.

Once I got to nineteen, I had some semblance of control, and lucky for me, when I turned around, she'd covered her bruises. Or, maybe it was lucky for Officer Rogers.

The man was dead. I didn't care what I had to do, I'd beat the shit out of him before the night was through.

Nobody laid their hands on my woman, not like that. And if they did, they had to face the consequences.

No matter what.

I gave her the calm that she thought she needed, however. I let her think that I was back in control, when in reality I was in the red zone.

"Where do you want to go eat?" I teased lightly.

I could eat, too.

It'd been a while since I'd had something, and I'd need my strength to beat the living shit out of that asshole, Rogers.

Little fucker.

"I'd like to go to El Hat," she said.

I winced.

I hated that restaurant. And it wasn't 'El Hat.' It was 'El Sombrero' but everyone in the entire city called it 'El Hat' for some reason.

The seating was too cramped, and I couldn't fucking breathe without blowing over the salt shaker on the next table.

"Okay," I shrugged. If that's where she wanted to eat, that's where we'd go.

She held out my spare key and smiled apologetically. "I didn't know what else to do."

Before she could get in, though, I stopped her by placing one hand on her belly and pushing her against the truck door.

"I don't care what you have to do to make sure that you're safe," I told her. "Even if you have to burn down the whole town around you. You're safe and that's all that matters to me. Got me?"

She blinked, and then nodded, eyes wide and—need I say it— turned on. "Yeah, I got it."

Her voice was husky and sweet, causing a little bit more of my control to unravel.

"I fucking love you, you know," I told her.

Her eyes were smiling as she said, "I love you, too, Evander Lennox. So freakin' much."

I meant to give her a sweet kiss. One that wouldn't get us in trouble for public indecency.

But that sweet kiss turned into a straight-up ravaging the moment I touched my mouth down to hers, and she went wild in my arms.

The only thing that caused me to pull away from her, even for a second, was the amused throat that cleared directly behind me.

I looked over my shoulder and saw Rafe standing there.

"I have news."

I growled.

"I have to take Kennedy to eat, then we'll meet at the club."

He shrugged. "I'm not really a team player yet. I'd rather give this to you now and have you take that information over."

I looked back at Kennedy.

"You mind if he comes with us?"

Her smile was delicate at best.

"Not at all."

I dropped another kiss to her mouth. "It'll be okay, baby."

She looked away. "Sure, it will."

***

Two hours later, I was full of chicken fajitas and white cheese queso, staring at the bowl of dwindling chips with a worried expression.

"So you're telling me that Balthazar had exotic peacocks…and that that dog killed the peacocks, too?"

Rafe nodded. "Information I'm getting from his two men, yeah. He went over there to confront her, just like you did. Gave him the same bitchy attitude."

"You give this information to the cops?"

Rafe looked at me, and then over to Kennedy, who was still shoveling food into her mouth from her plate. Rice and beans. *Yuck.*

Assured that she wasn't paying as much attention as she would have normally if we had her full attention, I nodded at Rafe to continue.

"You know I can't do that," he muttered. "Part of the gig."

Rafe wasn't here for just me. He was here for a few things. One of those things was a lot bigger fish than Balthazar.

Balthazar was a tiny little guppy compared to the massive, five-hundred-pound tuna that he was after—whatever that may be.

I gritted my teeth.

"Well, how do you suggest I get this information to the right people?"

"Call your brother."

I looked over to Kennedy, who was no longer eating, and grimaced.

My apologetic eyes flicked up to Rafe, and I winced.

He shrugged it off.

But I knew that shrug wasn't a throw-away move. He trusted me to take care of her and, essentially, him.

If she told the wrong people that Rafe wasn't just here to help out at Hail Auto Recovery, people would start asking questions. Questions led to answers. Answers led to death.

It was a vicious cycle, and I wouldn't put Rafe in danger like that. Not when he'd had my back when nobody else did.

Still did.

He was putting his own mission in jeopardy to ensure that I got out of this whole fuckin' mess unscathed, and I wouldn't let him down by allowing Kennedy to do anything that could possibly harm him. Even inadvertently.

"Okay," I said. "Why my brother?"

I didn't like talking to my brother. Talking to my brother led to me getting angry, and I'd already had one too many visits with jail this week.

The old feeling of claustrophobia had reared its ugly head while I'd been in there for those few hours, and it'd been enough to remind me that I didn't want to do that shit again. I'd run away to Mexico or fuckin' Timbuktu if I had to in order to stay out of jail.

The only problem now was that I would have to take someone with me.

But I could do it.

I always had a backup plan.

It was funny that Rafe and Kennedy had mentioned who the rest of the boys had brought in. Silas, the man who was offering up whatever information he could dig up on Balthazar and the police chief was the same man who had helped me with my backup plan— the one that was going to get Kennedy and I out of the country if it ever became necessary.

I just hoped that I never had to use that plan, because using that plan meant never coming back, and despite the fact that my family was all a bunch of assholes, I would still worry about them.

"Your brother, I think, saw the error of his ways," she wiped up what was left of the sour cream from her enchiladas with one finger. She brought the white cream to her mouth and licked her finger clean before continuing. "He wants to help, even though he's not sure how."

I gritted my teeth against the moan that threatened to spill from my lips at the sight of her licking her finger clean.

"Goddamn," Rafe muttered, looking away.

I grinned at him.

Kennedy had no fucking clue what she did to people. Even a man like Rafe; a man I'd never seen with another woman in the entire ten years that I'd known him, wasn't immune to her innocent little move.

"I'll call him. Give him the information," I cleared my throat and stood up. "Thanks for all that you gave us, Rafe."

Rafe wasn't stupid.

He knew that I was more than affected by Kennedy's impromptu show.

"But wait, I haven't eaten my sherbet yet!"

I looked down at the colorful frozen dessert that the waiter had put down in front of her the minute that I'd paid the check and picked up one of the spoons that hadn't been used. "It's to-go sherbet, now."

Then I hauled her up by her hand and pulled her in my wake, all the while listening to Rafe's chuckling laughter behind us.

"Evander," Kennedy said, tugging lightly on her arm. "What are you doing?"

I pulled her with me until we were out the door.

The moment that we were buried in the shadows of the building, I pushed her up against the brick wall and dropped my mouth down onto hers.

Again, it was only meant to be something short and sweet, but the moment my lips touched hers, I forgot all about short and sweet. All I wanted was her. All I tasted was her. All I craved was her.

Her hands went to my shoulders, and one of those shapely legs lifted to curl around my hip.

I dropped one of my hands to that leg and leaned into her, allowing her to feel what she did to me.

"We're leaving." I told her, breathless from the kiss. "You fuckin' kill me."

She gasped when I ground against her once more before pulling away.

"What brought this on?" she breathed heavily, pressing the sherbet cup to her chest and drawing it along the tops of both breasts.

I watched her, and then grinned.

"Get on my bike."

I was glad that the truck was switched out for my bike. The idea of her pressing up against me was highly appealing.

CHAPTER 25

I think the heat index is somewhere between OMG and WTF.
-Texas Facts

Kennedy

I'll never, ever, ever look at a cup of sherbet without thinking about the last three hours ever again.

No, not after what Evander had just done to me.

At first, I hadn't realized just how little Evander was in control until we got to the stoplight right outside of the restaurant.

I'd innocently started stroking his abs, burying my face in between his shoulder blades.

I loved his motorcycle. I'd also begged him to go get it before dinner, thinking that after we were done eating, we could go for a ride.

And that'd been my every intention, but the moment we'd left the restaurant, I knew that Evander had no intention of going anywhere but home.

Why?

Because I could practically feel the sexual tension leeching off of him.

Thinking to soothe that burn in him, as well as me, I'd slid my hand up and under his shirt, allowing the nails of one hand to trail down over his abs.

It'd been almost innocent, but the surprising reaction from him had set me back on my ass. Or would have had he not held onto my hair.

At first, I thought he was only going to return the loving gesture, but then he'd surprised me by shooting his hand out and grabbing hold of my hair, roughly bringing my mouth down to his in a kiss that went on so long that the people in the car behind us had to honk to let us know that the light had turned green.

After he'd let me go, he'd pulled through the intersection just in time for it to turn yellow, causing all four of the cars behind us to miss the light.

I'd giggled, dropping my head to his shoulder, and he'd latched onto my knee with one hand and held on for the duration of the ride.

Once we'd arrived at his house, he pulled the bike into the car port beside the side door.

I could hear Gertie barking to be let out the moment he shut the motor off, and just as I moved to dismount, he growled something.

I felt my body moving and found myself sitting on the gas tank in front of him.

Then my shirt was ripped off over my head, and my bra was being yanked down.

The next thing to happen was his mouth finding the sensitive peak of my nipple as he sucked it inside his hot mouth. My eyes rolled back in my head, and my back arched, urging him to take more of me.

Which he did, sucking my nipple into his mouth completely and giving it a few hard tugs.

My hands went to his hair as I searched for something to hold onto.

And then he bit down.

It wasn't too hard, but it was enough to have my pussy spasming as desire shot through my body.

"Oh, God," I breathed out shakily.

All of that from just a little nipple play.

Though, sitting on the back of his bike, pressed in close to him while his bike vibrated beneath me was likely also a contributing factor.

Whatever the reason, I was so gone for him that I didn't realize he was pulling his zipper down until I felt him wrap my hand around his hard cock.

I clenched onto him, automatically starting to work his cock in time to his sucks on my nipple.

The abrasive rasp of his beard against the sensitive flesh was also really doing it for me. The entire situation, right down to his hauling me around bodily to the front of his bike, was so much of a turn on that I didn't realize I was only moments away from an orgasm until I was already falling over the edge.

It was enough to steal my breath.

"Fuck me," he growled. "You just came?"

I blinked open my eyes, unaware that I'd stopped working his cock, and nodded.

"Fuck yeah," he growled.

Then I found myself standing beside the bike.

"Take off your jeans."

I didn't hesitate.

I only shoved them down over my hips—without unbuttoning them, might I add—and kicked off my tennis shoes all in the same moment.

Before I could ask him what was next, he picked me back up around the waist, this time my back to his front, and he sat me down onto his lap.

His cock was trapped between our bodies, and I began to writhe in his lap in attempt to urge him to hurry.

"You remember what we talked about earlier?" he asked. "When I came to get you?"

I licked my lips.

"About you wanting me pregnant?" I confirmed.

I wasn't so sure about that.

I'd never thought of myself as mom material, but I'd do damn near anything for this man, even bear his children out of wedlock if he wanted me to.

"I want them," he growled.

He lifted me slightly to reposition me over his cock, my breasts pressed to the cool metal, as he stood behind me.

"I'd do damn near anything to see you swollen with my child," he murmured against my neck, lining his cock up to my entrance.

I bit my lip and looked at him over my shoulder.

The only light offered was from the motion-activated flood lights that were shining on his front yard, but it was just enough to allow me to see the veins in his hands throbbing. I could also see the determined expression on his face.

I closed my eyes when I felt that thick head pressing into me.

"Fuck," he hissed, pausing after he'd barely breached my entrance. "Forgot how tight you are."

And then he sank inside, one slow inch at a time, until his balls were pressed against my skin.

I could feel the rasp of his pubic hair on my ass and legs, and I was panting with how full he made me feel.

And that's about the time that I felt the first drip of cold sherbet slowly making its way down my exposed breasts.

I looked up to find him tilting the little plastic cup over my left breast.

Drip. Drip. Drip.

One drop hit my nipple and slid down. The next hit me along the outside of my breast, curling around it and rolling all the way down to my side.

The last fell between my breasts, traveling down my body, around my navel, and disappearing into my pubic hair.

I closed my eyes and swallowed.

I was just about to compose myself—somewhat—when I felt a cold drop hit my clit.

My eyes shot open, and I stared, open mouthed, at the man holding the container of sherbet right above my clit.

"Bet that tastes divine," he growled, dropping his finger and swiping away all evidence of the melted dessert that was on the tip of my nipple.

My pussy contracted around his cock, causing him to groan.

"Fuck yes," he growled, then forgot all about the ice cream as he reached to pull me closer.

The only problem with that was that he dropped the ice cream onto me, spilling the partially frozen dessert straight in my lap, making the cold, melted goodness spill all over the both of us directly where we were connected.

Did he care, though?

No.

Why?

Because he'd lost any semblance of control.

He took me like a man possessed.

At first, he allowed me to act like I had some say in the way he was fucking me. But soon he was controlling all my movements with his big hands that were clamped around my hips. He rocked me hard and fast on his cock. I just grabbed onto his forearms and dropped my head back to rest against his shoulder.

My breasts were flopping a bit uncomfortably with his rough movements, and to communicate this, I dug my nails into the muscles of his forearms.

But then he changed the angle and started to hit that spot.

The one that changed everything and made all the difference in the world.

The fat, engorged head of him tapped against *it*, fast at first, and then he slowed until the tip dragged over it with each thrust. Over and over and over again.

It was enough to cause something inside of me to change…there was this urge. One I'd never felt before, and I damn near exploded right out of my skin.

He snaked an arm around my waist to keep moving me while one of the hands that had been digging into my hips trailed over my belly. With his thumb and forefinger, he reached down and pinched my clit, sending me detonating into the next time zone.

If Evander had neighbors, I would've been worried.

My scream was loud and terrifying.

But the orgasm he gave me? *So much more.*

I clenched around him, pulsing and coaxing the same in return from him.

And I got it, too.

Moments later he came, his muscles contracting. His arms squeezed me tighter as his entire body grew rigid while he grunted out his release.

A release that I felt as it splashed inside of me, filling me up so full that I could've sworn that there was likely no more room inside of me.

"I think," I panted, "That you broke me."

He grunted something in reply, and then easily stood with me still impaled on him and hanging over his arms like some exhausted spider monkey.

Our bodies slid together, as our commingled releases—as well as the melted sherbet—coated both of our bodies.

"At least it's not in my hair."

He grunted. "Guess that's good."

I started to laugh, and then I pulled his face down to mine.

"I'm glad you're home."

He pushed open the door to his house, moved to the side to let Gertie out, and then returned the kiss.

"Anywhere you are, baby." he growled. "Home is where you are, and always will be."

My eyes filled with tears.

"What are we going to do?"

His arms tightened.

"We'll figure it out…tomorrow," he replied, disengaging his body from mine. "Tonight, all I want to do is sleep in my own bed, with you in my arms."

I'd give him tonight.

Tomorrow I'd worry about him. Tomorrow I'd worry about how I was going to make a living. Tomorrow, everything would be resolved…I just knew it.

CHAPTER 26

Don't break anybody's heart. They only have one. Break bones instead. They have two hundred and six.
-True shit

Evander

"Oh, shit," Kennedy breathed. "Look."

I let my gaze drift to where she was pointing and winced.

An officer was there, his squad car back behind him about a hundred yards, with a man about three times his size straddling his chest. The man was pounding his fist into the officer's face, and I mentally calculated how many times it would take a punch to the head before the officer passed out for good.

"Goddammit," I growled, shoving the kickstand down and getting off my bike. "Stay here. And call the cops."

Kennedy nodded mutely, staying where she was straddling my bike, and staring at the commotion happening in front of her.

I stomped across the street, flipping off a driver who'd honked at me when I'd been nowhere near close enough for him to hit me, and kept walking.

"Watch where you're going, motherfucker."

I turned my glare to the man who'd popped his fat head out of the window to let him see just how unhappy I was.

The driver swallowed, ducked back into his car and peeled away as fast as his Honda Civic would take him.

It didn't take me long to realize that the officer getting his ass kicked was none other than my brother.

But, regardless of my feelings toward the dumb bastard, I wouldn't allow him to get his ass kicked.

Not now, not ever.

Which was why I walked up to the man straddling him, yanked him up by his collar, and bodily threw him straight into the open squad car's backseat.

He hit the other side of the car with a loud thump, and before he could make it back to his feet, I slammed the door shut.

I stared down at my brother, watching him pant, as blood dripped down his face out of his nose.

"You okay?" I asked him.

My brother nodded, wincing slightly when he did.

"Yeah," he croaked. "Just fucking dandy."

I stared down at him.

"I was trying to call you," I informed him.

He huffed out a short breath, then rolled over to his side, and then more slowly up to his knees.

"I was a little busy," he admitted. "What did you want?"

I shoved both hands into my pocket.

"Sources in Balthazar's employ say he went a little mad when his prized peacocks were eaten by his neighbor's dog. He went to confront her and one thing led to another."

Walter's blood shot eyes came to me.

"You think that Balthazar killed a woman over his freakin' peacocks?" he clarified, wiping blood away from the corner of his lip.

I shrugged. "What reason did they give you as to why I did it?"

I mean, it was Kennedy's chickens that had been killed and they weren't prized, but they were her sole source of income.

Sure, they made her money, but I didn't have the same attachment to her then as I did now.

Not to mention they weren't even mine.

I would have no reason to bring harm to that woman.

"Your dog."

I looked over at my bike, thinking about Gertie, and shrugged. "No harm there. I had an ironclad contract when it came to Gertie. Not to mention there's probably a gazillion cameras in that state of the art facility of hers. If they wanted to know what exactly went down, then they'd pull the feed."

Walter grunted something unintelligible. "Whatever. I'm just going off of what I hear, and nobody would shoot another person over a fucking peacock. Guaran-damn-tee it."

With nothing left to say to that, I left him to it and walked back to my motorcycle, wondering idly if my brother should even be considered a brother if he didn't even like me.

I mean, at what point did a brother become a brother, and not just a sibling?

I would trust the boys at HAR—Hail Auto Recovery—with my life. Would I trust Walter?

Turns out, it was a good thing that I didn't trust him.

Seems that the chief of police wasn't the only one who was dirty.

CHAPTER 27

*What's right isn't always legal, and what's legal
isn't always right.*

-Evander to Kennedy

Evander

Kennedy was riding my cock. She was seconds away from coming. I could feel the rippling of her pussy as she started over that peak.

I was letting her do all the work, my hands fisted behind my head, as I watched her take what she needed.

Her breasts were jolting with each slam of her hips, and I was counting to one hundred in my head to keep myself from coming before her.

I was doing a shitty job of it, too.

If she didn't hurry, I'd come without her.

Literally, blow everything before she even crested.

In fact, I was focused on ignoring the way she was slamming down on me, giving me everything that she had to give, when I heard the sound.

A sound that one shouldn't hear in the dead of night.

I'd woken Kennedy up around two in the morning after I'd felt her ass pushing up against my cock for over an hour.

Finally giving up, I'd rolled her over on top of me, and then fitted my cock to her entrance.

Which led us to now, her still riding me, and me hearing a noise.

It sounded like a door opening.

One that I didn't use every day, because it creaked slightly, and thankfully so, since it was now alerting me to the fact that someone was entering into my domain.

Gertie must've heard it, too, because he started barking.

At first, it was just an alert bark—kind of like, Hey! I heard that!

But then it turned into something more sinister. Into something that was akin to "you shouldn't fucking be in here."

The barks were ferocious, and I had Kennedy rolled off of me and pushed to the floor within seconds.

All my honed instincts from my military days and then from my auto-recovery days, had me on my feet, sliding my pants on and reaching for my gun in under ten seconds.

Only, I no longer had a gun.

I had a fucking baseball bat.

There were two fucking things that you didn't do when you were in a gunfight.

One, you didn't pursue if you didn't have anything adequate to protect yourself.

Two, you didn't bring a knife—or a fucking baseball bat—because that was the first thing that would get you killed.

"Call the cops," I ordered, then opened the door and closed it just as quietly.

She didn't argue, and I could hear her scrambling behind me. Then I cursed.

If I could hear her, that would mean that someone else could hear her, too.

I backed into the shadows of the hallway and stepped quietly, sticking to the side and letting my back just barely skim against the wall so I didn't hit anything that Kennedy and I had left when we'd gotten home yesterday.

Like our clothes and our shoes.

A hoarse curse, followed by a short bark of gunfire, had me moving faster.

The most eerie thing was the utter silence that followed.

No more barking. No more movement.

No nothing.

And I knew.

Gertie wouldn't have stopped barking.

He wouldn't.

Sick to my stomach, I finally hit the end of the hallway and glanced around.

There was nothing there.

At least not at first glance.

My eyes were adjusted to the darkness, but there was enough moonlight shining through the curtains of the living room for me to see that there was a large black lump on the ground next to the couch.

There was also somebody sitting in my chair.

"Turn on the lights and join me."

I knew that voice.

It was one that would haunt me for the rest of my life.

The man who had been responsible for framing me for a crime that I did not commit.

"I can see you. I have night vision eyewear on," Balthazar drawled the moment I'd started to move. "Now, come out from behind that wall or I'll have my associate kill the woman."

I swallowed thickly and stepped out, knowing from some sort of sixth sense that he wasn't joking.

He had someone in the house with him, and somehow, some way, he'd gotten that associate in without me realizing it.

"I've taken care of the leaks in my organization," he said the moment I reached for the lights. "Thank your source for rectifying one of my problems for me. It's hard to know who tells what lies. Though, it's true that my prized peacocks were killed, only one man knew that. Now that man is no longer in my employ."

I growled under my breath and tried not to freak the fuck out.

Then, hoping I was right and he hadn't taken the goggles off, I flipped the lights on and started to move.

All at once I flew into action, and I was rewarded for my quick actions.

Balthazar doubled over as he practically yanked the glasses off his face and threw them to the ground in his haste to get them free.

I knew the feeling.

It hurt like a son of a bitch to have happen.

"The only problem with the infrared night vision goggles?" I growled, hefting my bat. "Is that you have to adjust your eyesight. Fuckin' hurts to have light added to your vision with those bad boys on, doesn't it?"

Then I swung my bat, hitting Balthazar straight across the side of his head.

He slumped down into the chair like he'd had his strings cut, and I turned to go back to Kennedy.

Only, the moment I stepped a foot in the direction of her, my front door was kicked in and Detective Mueller was there.

"Drop the weapon!" he screamed.

I dropped the bat and gestured to the hallway, wary of the gun that the detective had pointed at me.

"Get on the ground," he ordered, gesturing to the ground.

I'd been avoiding the ground.

Looking at the ground was admitting to myself that Gertie was gone, and I refused to do that right then.

In a while, once I was sure that Kennedy was okay, then I'd confront one of my worst fears.

Then, I'd look.

Right now? No, I was not getting on the ground.

"There's someone else in the house with my fiancé," I told Mueller. "He's in my bedroom. She's in there, likely naked and vulnerable, and I'm not leaving her to whomever has her."

Mueller stared at me, gauging my sincerity, and nodded once.

He moved past me down my hallway, shuffling his feet and making so much goddamn noise that I wanted to pull my hair out.

The man was inexperienced, and I had no doubt in my mind that he was about to kill not just himself, but me and Kennedy right along with him.

I was right behind him, ready to intervene if I was needed with my bat, and wasn't prepared.

Not for what I saw the moment that the door was thrown open by Mueller.

First rule in combat, always be prepared.

Mueller hadn't even anticipated the shot that came at him before he threw the door open.

Hell, he'd just stood there like a goddamn idiot.

The lucky thing for him—and for me—was that he was about half a foot shorter than me, something that, unfortunately for the man who was holding my woman, he hadn't expected.

And Walter had wasted his shot.

He'd thought that it was me, and he'd aimed high.

Mueller returned fire in the next instant, making my heart leap straight out of my chest.

I wasn't confident in his detective skills, and I sure as fuck wasn't confident in his hostage negotiation skills.

But the man was nothing if not lucky.

He took one shot, and that one shot missed Kennedy's face by less than an inch.

Nobody would've ever taken that shot on the fly like Mueller had without first taking the time to aim.

No, not Mueller.

He just shot at hip level and let it fly, nearly losing his head when I barely corralled the urge to aim my bat at the stupid fucker's head.

My brother hit the floor with a meaty thud, and Kennedy went right along with him, the weight of his body still holding onto hers and taking her down whether she wanted to go or not.

But she didn't stay there for long. Moments after hitting the floor, she was scrambling away, heading straight for me.

Mueller walked over to the dead man, nearly stepping on Kennedy's fingers, and pressed his hand to Walter's neck.

"Shit, he's gone."

He picked up the gun that Walter had in his hand before he fell, and then shoved it into the waistband of his jeans.

"You okay?" he asked Kennedy, who'd finally arrived at my feet and crawled her way into my arms.

I was shaking.

I couldn't breathe.

And I was seconds away from beating the living shit out of Mueller.

Literally, if there wasn't so much wrong with this situation, I would've beat the man to death until there was absolutely nothing left of him that was recognizable.

That's when I became aware that we weren't alone in the house any longer.

Which was a good thing, because I was an instant away from losing my shit.

That, and Kennedy was losing it in my arms.

"Oh, God," she whispered over and over. "Oh, God. Oh, God. I'm so sorry, Evander. Oh, God."

I squeezed her tighter.

"Get down on the ground!"

That was the chief of police.

Just fucking lovely.

"I said get down on the ground!"

That's when I realized that he was talking to me.

***

"Sir, my client was in his own home. In his bed. Practically naked." My new lawyer, some hot shot from a few towns over named Todd something or other, growled at the chief of police. "He's, in fact, still in his underwear. You haven't given him food or water in over seven hours, and you're violating so many of his rights here that I don't even know where to start."

I agreed.

Yet I kept my mouth shut.

"I've got a few men that want to have a chat with you."

That was news to me.

I glanced at the door when it was opened, surprised to see three large men standing there.

Rafe was one of them. With him was an older man with a fan-fucking-tastic beard and another male who looked ready to rip everyone's head off.

"What kind of horse crap is this?" Fowler seethed, standing up so abruptly that his seat behind him hit the wall with a crack. "This is my fucking police station. Get out!"

Rafe stepped inside and shook his head, eyeing Fowler like he was unimpressed.

It was, indeed, his police station. But it wouldn't be for much longer. I wasn't sure that Fowler had ever seen that particular side of the interrogation room table.

"Actually," Rafe drawled. "This is no longer your police station. As of right now, the Texas Rangers have opened a corruption investigation of this office and all officers associated with it due to the recent events. There is no longer a functional police station in the city of Hostel."

Fowler's face went beet red.

"You can't…"

"No, but I can."

A Texas Ranger in full uniform walked straight up to Fowler and held out his hand. "Pending the outcome of this investigation, you are officially relieved of duty until such a time as you are either exonerated of the charges that have been leveled against this office or you are otherwise deemed fit for duty."

I knew that wasn't going to happen.

Any decent investigator would see this farce of a police department as the fucking den of dishonesty that it is.

Hell, I hadn't even been here for the last four years—although I did have first-hand knowledge of how corrupt these cops were, seeing as I went to jail either because of their inability to adequately conduct an investigation or, even worse, their role in framing me for this crime.

I also now knew that there were at least two dirty police officers in Balthazar's pockets. My brother and Fowler.

"You can't…"

The Texas Ranger grinned. "I just did."

And that was that.

Lani Lynn Vale

CHAPTER 28

If a boy gives you butterflies, your heart is in danger.
-Fact of Life

Kennedy

I dug a hole in the ground.

My hands were blistered. One finger was bleeding due to a splinter, but I wouldn't stop until the hole was big enough.

I hiccupped on a sob as I scooped out another shovelful of dirt.

"Would you please, for the love of all that's holy, let me help you?"

I shook my head at Rafe's insistence and kept scooping.

The hole I was digging was large, but it wasn't large enough.

Not to hold a deceased dog of Gertie's size.

"God, this is the hardest thing in the world to watch."

I glanced up to see that I'd gained another man in my audience.

This one was a man in full uniform.

A Texas Ranger, if I had to guess.

"That's what I've been saying for the last hour," Rafe grumbled to himself. "You get Evander home?"

"I did," the Texas Ranger confirmed. "He was released on his own recognizance about half an hour ago. Though, I don't think that he knows that his woman is out here doing this, or he wouldn't have insisted on going to the hospital looking for her."

I frowned. "Why does he think I'm at the hospital?"

The Texas Ranger looked at me. "Apparently, you were supposed to be there undergoing some tests."

I had been...over two hours ago. Now I was here, doing this.

"Rafe?"

Rafe looked at me, his gaze unwavering.

"Yeah?"

"If I let you finish, will you go pick up Evander and bring him back here?"

Rafe nodded, looking relieved.

"Yeah."

I let the shovel drop from my limp hands, and then sat on the edge of the hole and waited.

Rafe disappeared sometime later, and I could tell that men were still surrounding me.

At some point, two got into the hole and started digging around me.

They made short work of it.

Made it look so much easier than I had.

I didn't care, though.

I didn't speak.

I only waited.

It wasn't long.

Maybe fifteen minutes at most.

I heard the motorcycle before I saw it, and then turned my head to watch as Evander came barreling around the curve of the driveway. He came to a stop directly in front of where I'd been digging, and then threw his leg over the bike before marching toward me.

I stood up, and with very little effort on his part, he hauled me up into his arms and buried his face in my neck.

"Are you okay?" I asked him shakily.

He didn't reply, only squeezed tighter.

I wasn't sure whether to take that as a yes or a no.

"I was digging a g-g-grave," I said. "For Gertie."

Evander's big body shuddered.

He still didn't reply.

"Do you want me to get them to bring him out here?"

He couldn't stay in there much longer.

His large body had been covered with a sheet in the middle of the living room.

Unfortunately, with everything else that was going on, including Evander's house being a crime scene, I couldn't do any more until they'd officially released it back to us.

And that hadn't been for another eight, long hours.

If we had waited much longer, it would have begun to smell.

And I didn't want Evander to remember Gertie like that.

"I'll get him."

"No," I refused to let Evander see him.

It was bad.

Really bad.

"I'll do it," Travis muttered.

Then he was gone.

And I held onto Evander as he tried to pull away.

"Please?"

Evander's face lifted, and he stared into my eyes.

Something in them must've struck home, because he nodded and waited.

Travis appeared moments later, the black draped form cradled in his arms.

His muscles were straining and veins were pulsing in his neck.

Gertie was heavy.

Travis never once uttered a sound.

Not when he stepped down into the hole.

Not when he gently squatted down.

And not when he laid the unmoving form into the hole I'd half dug.

Evander pulled away from me and looked down into the hole.

His shoulders were slumped, and he was staring down into it like his heart was breaking.

I took hold of his hand and brought it up to my mouth, placing a single kiss to the knuckles before tucking the big hand into my chest and clutching it tightly.

"Please cover him up."

Those were the last words Evander said the rest of the night.

***

Two days later

A lot had happened in two days.

The Texas Ranger, Griffin Storm, had shut down the Hostel Police Department.

Until a special election could be held to elect a new police chief, no one would set foot inside of the station again.

The information that a computer analyst had been able to scrounge up on not only Fowler, but also Walter and Balthazar, had been pretty damn impressive.

The man, Jack from a business called Free, had gathered the information in less than eighteen hours.

His partner and wife, Winter, had also been a major player in finding the information.

Using the information he'd been provided, Texas Ranger Griffin Storm had decided that Fowler not only wouldn't be getting his job back, but he'd also be facing charges—and a lot of them.

Some of those charges related to his involvement in manufacturing charges that led to the false imprisonment a man following a conviction for crimes that he did not commit—that man being *my* man.

Another man named Wolf—Travis' former brother-in-law—had also arrived. He'd put his skills to use and had focused in on Evander's brother, Walter.

After a search of his home, as well as an examination of his cell phone records and eyewitness accounts, it was determined that Walter had been in cahoots with Balthazar—providing him with information and services that only a dirty police officer could provide.

And Balthazar's one remaining employee, a man named Ramirez, had copped a plea, according to Travis's understanding.

All of the information we received was secondhand, and only came to me by way of Rafe and Travis, who came by daily to check on Evander. An Evander who'd done nothing but remain silent over the last few days.

I'd stayed at Evander's side through all of it—learning that his brother was dirty. Learning that he'd been exonerated of all the charges that he had been convicted of previously, thanks to information that was gained from the statement that Ramirez gave when he took his plea deal. And finally, when he learned that the State of Texas would be contacting him to discuss compensation for falsely imprisoning him.

Which had been a hard pill to swallow.

Ramirez could've just as easily given up this information four years ago, keeping Evander out of prison.

But he hadn't, and now a man had four years of his life stolen from him, and there wasn't a damn thing that would ever make that acceptable, not even a payout from the state.

"Is there anything else?" I asked Rafe.

Rafe looked at me, studying my eyes, and then shook his head.

"Went over to your place and cleaned up," he hesitated. "Took care of the animals again. Brought them over to Travis' place, though. Didn't think bringing the dog here would be smart."

Rafe's call on that was a good one.

Evander was devastated.

He was lost without Gertie, and I couldn't blame him.

"I have something else I have to take care of, and I likely won't be back in town for about two weeks. That leaves the crew shorthanded with Evander out, too." He weighed what he had to say next. "I think you should tell him he's needed at work. Maybe returning to his normal routine will help."

I doubted it, but I'd try.

I'd do anything for Evander.

Lani Lynn Vale

CHAPTER 29

Someone asked me where I saw myself in ten years. I told them I didn't even know what I wanted to make for dinner.
-Text from Kennedy to Evander

Kennedy

Three weeks later

Everything was back to normal—or at least as normal as you could get.

Hostel was a small town.

It hadn't taken long for the town to learn that Evander had been innocent of all charges.

It'd taken even less time for them to hear that Evander had beaten someone to death with a baseball bat—though beaten was a strong word. Really, he'd just hit him, but it'd been enough to kill him in one blow. It didn't matter to the town that Balthazar was a drug-dealing pimp, and had been in his house uninvited and had just shot his dog when Evander had done the deed.

They still saw him as the enemy.

And I was fucking tired of it.

Evander may be going through the motions—working and participating in life—but he wasn't back to normal yet.

And that was in evidence now.

There I was, standing in the middle of the supermarket aisle where the pregnancy tests were located, and I was listening to some woman whisper about Evander.

Evander was at the end of the aisle looking at something, unaware that I was looking at pregnancy tests and wondering if I could sneak it into the cart without him noticing it.

He was only a few feet away from the two women—both baseball moms who obviously couldn't help themselves—as they talked about him as if he wasn't standing right there.

And I finally lost it.

Marching down the aisle—four pregnancy tests still in my hands— I started yelling.

"Don't you fucking see?" I screeched, throwing the tests at the two women. "This man is so fucking perfect. He has the patience of a saint and all y'all can fuckin' do is talk about him like he's a fucking criminal. Well, guess what, bitches? He fucking isn't! He's a good, honest, hard-working man who was targeted by a dirty police force. He hasn't done a damn thing to deserve the asshole attitude y'all are dishing out to him," I huffed out a humorless laugh. "Fuck y'all. Fuck you and fuck you." I threw my last pregnancy test at them and hit the blonde in the side of her shocked face. "Just go fuck yourselves."

Okay.

I could tell that I wasn't as eloquent in my wording as I probably could have been, but I was so tired of it that I couldn't hold it in any longer.

The two women just stared at me in shock.

Evander, the loving, gentle giant that he was, just bent over and picked up the box that had bounced close to his feet after hitting the other chick on the neck.

He read the box and then turned those beautiful eyes up to me.

"You have something to tell me?"

I gritted my teeth.

And then I started to cry.

"I have a lot to tell you."

Then buried my face in my hands and let all of the emotion of the last few weeks rush out. All the grief, the sadness, my worry for him.

All of it came tumbling out.

"I'm sorry."

Two words.

But they were apparently exactly what I needed to hear.

"It's okay."

"It's not," he countered. "And for what it's worth, I'm thankful that you gave me this time, but I'm sorry that doing it hurt you."

His repeated words had me bringing up my head.

"I know."

He dropped his mouth to mine, and then wrapped his arms carefully around me.

"You're pregnant?"

I shrugged, leaning my head back to stare into his eyes.

"I don't know."

He threw the box into the cart and then let go of me, but only long enough to pull me with him back to the other end of the aisle.

He stopped long enough to grab four more boxes, and then he calmly walked with me to the front of the store.

There, he unloaded our purchases, paid for them and then walked me out.

All without saying a word.

In fact, the silence continued until we got home, where he opened the boxes and then held one out to me as he guided me into the bathroom. "All right, time to pee."

I balked.

"I can't pee with you standing right here."

He held out the stick, jiggling it in my face.

"Pee."

I sighed, took the wand from him, and then did the deed.

All while blushing profusely as he stood over me and calmly waited for me to finish.

I set the test on the counter, finished up, washed my hands, and then shifted nervously from foot-to-foot.

He wrapped his arms around me from behind, as we both watched the pink plus sign rapidly appearing in the tiny window.

The big man at my back buried his face into my neck and started to laugh.

"We're going to have a baby."

I nodded, staring at him like he'd lost his marbles—which I was sure that he had.

"What's wrong with you?" I asked when he wiped the tears from the corners of his eyes.

He was laughing so hard he was crying.

Holy shit, something was wrong.

The man had literally gone crazy.

"What are you laughing about?" I repeated, worried now.

He grinned, then pulled me into his arms again and touched the test almost reverently.

"I'm...happy."

I frowned.

"A lot of shit has happened," he said. "I've lost a brother. My dog. My sister fucking hates me now...but I'm so fucking happy."

I stayed silent.

"Don't worry about me anymore, K."

I snorted.

"No," he repeated, curling his hand around my jaw. "I'll get there, but in the meantime, I need you to keep being you."

I could do that.

"Okay?"

I did the only thing I could do. I nodded.

"As long as you love me," he continued. "As long as you're there when I wake up in the morning. As long as you're here when I get home at night." He pressed a kiss to my lips. "As long as you're in my life, then I can do just about anything."

With that, he walked out of the room, and I was left standing in the middle of the bathroom, my heart overflowing with joy.

"As long as you love me, I'll do the same for you."

What he said in a shout from the other room, however, had me nearly squealing with happiness.

"And you'll be marrying me in two months, too! No lip!"

EPILOGUE

Of course, I have flaws, but my boobs normally distract people from them.
-Kennedy to Evander

Kennedy

"I can't believe he bought you a two-thousand-dollar bean bag as a wedding gift."

I looked over to the man who said that. Travis, Evander's boss.

I smiled at him in return, managing to make it only a little bit strained.

"It's the best thing you'll ever sit in," I told him. "Try it."

He looked at the huge, hulking blob in the middle of the floor, and immediately shook his head.

"I can't," he sighed. "I have to meet Hannah."

Hannah, the woman who had given birth to his child. The woman whom Travis loved but wouldn't be with due to some misguided loyalty to another woman.

I seriously felt awful for Hannah. Truly awful.

I knew how it felt to be second best, and my heart ached for her. The heartache on Hannah's face every time I saw her was enough to make my heart ache.

I hated it.

And I think I even hated Travis a little bit for it, too.

He'd been good to Evander. He'd saved my life. Hell, he was even going to be the godfather of our child, but I hated what he was doing to Hannah.

I hated it with a passion.

"Baby?"

I blinked, surprised to find Evander standing in front of me.

"Hey!" I said, smiling at my husband. "What's up?"

My husband.

We'd only been married four hours earlier, and we were now attending our wedding reception in the middle of the club owned by the Hails. I still hadn't met Dante yet, though.

I'd heard a lot about him, but he'd remained elusive to me.

"Yeah?" I grinned at him.

My eyes raked up and down his body.

God, he looked so good in a tux.

He'd surprised me by wearing one. I hadn't expected it of him.

In fact, as I'd been walking down the aisle, I'd been looking for the man wearing jeans and a lavender button-down shirt that I'd bought for him only yesterday.

What I hadn't been looking for was a man who was tall, dark and debonair in a three-piece suit.

Now, though, the jacket had been shed, which didn't surprise me.

He'd been sweating when I had made my way up aisle to him.

The club was hotter than hell, and I'd said as much in front of the preacher who married us.

He'd given me a raised eyebrow, and I'd slapped my hand over my mouth.

"Baby?"

I blinked, taken out of my contemplation of my man's assets.

"Yeah?" I repeated, this time actually paying attention.

"Your nephew is on the phone."

I blinked, surprised to find that he was.

I hadn't spoken to my nephews or my niece since my sister had died.

Not that I hadn't tried.

I'd tried a ton.

I'd called. Called my dad. Called my brother.

None of them had given me Darren's forwarding address, and none of them had told me where I could look for him.

In fact, Darren had even gone as far as to change his freakin' number.

Evander had said that he could find the number for me if I wanted it…and, one day, I would.

That day would be one year exactly from the day that Darren had ripped away all I had left of my family from me. That's when I'd ask for that number.

It hurt, but I was willing to make that sacrifice for the kids, even though he would never give me the same courtesy.

"Really?" I asked in awe.

He nodded, and then held out my phone to me.

I'd given it to him to hold since he had pockets, and I didn't. He'd been taking pictures with it of me and him, or of other random stuff that would make me smile later on, all night.

"Thank you," I whispered, taking the phone.

He winked at me and walked away, taking Travis with him.

I nervously placed the phone to my ear, and started to cry the moment I heard my sister's son's voice for the first time in what felt like forever.

Evander had done some digging into my past one fateful night my father had said a few choice words to me about how I 'wasn't good for nothin'.' From there, he discovered that our parents hadn't actually split their children evenly and that was that. Apparently, a long time ago, my father had tried to contact me for my brother. When I'd 'written' back, I'd explained to them that I wanted nothing to do with them.

Only, I hadn't written that letter. I hadn't even known a letter existed, or that my father had tried reaching out to me.

He'd shared this 'letter' that I'd written to him a few months after Trixie's death, then told me to leave. I'd taken one look at the handwriting and had known instantly that my mother had been the one behind it.

My 'letter' had also explained my brother's and sister's initial hesitancy toward me.

After explaining this to my father, he didn't believe me. So…I'd given up.

It wasn't worth my time, or my happiness, to tried to convince a stubborn old man that I wasn't the asshole that he thought I was. Especially when he wouldn't give me the time of day.

Though, every once in a while, I still tried to bridge that gap.

It never worked.

So, for now, I tried to be happy that my sister's children were allowed to contact me again.

It would have to be enough.

"I can't wait to tell you about the home run I hit!"

I grinned, stood in the middle of my wedding reception, cake in hand, and felt pure fucking happiness course through me. "I can't wait to listen."

Then I thanked my lucky stars as DJ promised that he'd call again tomorrow because his dad was tired of his 'insistent' whining.

Whatever. I'd take it.

I'd take anything Darren was willing to give.

***

Two hours later, it took both Evander and I to roll the huge bean bag into our living room.

We'd made the mistake of opening the enormous thing at the club. Then we tried to stuff it back into its bag—only getting part of it in there since there was no way in hell that the whole thing was going back in the bag no matter how hard we tried—so we could put it onto the flatbed part of Travis' tow truck for transport back to our place.

Travis had helped us get it to the front porch before he'd been called away on a recovery, leaving us to shove it through the front door of our house on our own.

Well…I'd helped push. Evander had gotten it in the most of the way before he had forced me to wait outside until he got it through the door.

"Now," he said as he walked over to me, bending at the waist and then lifting me up into his arms.

I squealed and threw my arms around his neck, holding on for dear life, even though I knew he wouldn't drop me.

"But we forgot to feed the goats!" I cried out.

I'd decided to hold off on getting more chickens, so the only farm animals I had at the moment were my goats and my dog.

My dog that still was a bit unsure about Evander and didn't try to hide it.

One day, I would get more chickens. One day, I would forget that Balthazar had ordered his minions over to my place to 'give a warning' that I hadn't heeded. That warning being that he decapitated every single chicken that I owned.

A warning that I hadn't realized was a warning. Ramirez, Balthazar's minion, had informed me that I'd gone to the police, which had expedited Balthazar's timetable—meaning that he'd taken the risk at visiting us himself, bringing Walter as backup. What he hadn't expected was such a fast response time by the police, or for Evander to have a freakin' bat.

"Don't worry about them," Evander growled against my neck. "Worry about me."

"You don't have anything that I need to worry about at this point…" I countered cheekily.

His mouth turned up into a grin. "No?"

I didn't like that grin. It was his 'I'm about to do something you won't like' grin.

Then he started toward my Lovesac.

"Evander, no," I growled. "We're not doing it on my Lovesac."

My precious baby that I'd seen on Facebook and had cost an arm and a leg. A beautiful piece of furniture that still didn't have a cover on it.

He ignored me.

Then started running to take a flying jump, with me in his arms curled around him like a monkey. He came down hard on the Lovesac, but I didn't so much as jolt.

The air left my lungs as my wedding present took the brunt of our fall.

"Goddammit, Evander!" I said, laughter tinging my voice. "What the hell are we supposed to do now?"

We were both sunk down in the beast of a bean bag. We were cocooned on all four sides, and it was glorious.

In a few months, however, when I was further along in my pregnancy, it would definitely be a bitch to get out of it.

"We're supposed to make love."

I laughed, thinking that he was joking.

We couldn't make love on my Lovesac! How cliché!

Except he was perfectly serious and went about showing me how very serious he was moments later.

By the time he was finished showing me, I was totally on board with Lovesac lovin'.

My face was buried in the canvas cloth, and my arms were sprawled out above my head.

The lower half of my body was supported by the rest of it.

I felt like a human hotdog.

"I brought a towel," he said, handing me the towel. "Grabbed it on the way over."

The minute I saw it, I shook my head. "I can't use that. I cleaned up bacon grease with it, not to mention that there's bleach and kitchen cleaner on that towel."

He flipped the towel over. "This side is dry."

I was already shaking my head. "No! I swear to God…do you know how bad yeast infections suck?"

He dropped his forehead to my shoulder.

"Well, I can't really just pull out. It'll go everywhere…including onto your Lovesac."

I immediately shot my hand down between my legs to hold him there as I started laughing.

He joined me, and we were both laughing so hard, tears were pouring out of my eyes.

"Oh, God," I wheezed. "Jesus."

I could feel his cock deflating inside of me as he laughed, and moments later, he slipped free.

I caught it as best as I could and started to roll as Evander went up on his knees.

That's when I got caught in a low spot in the bean bag. I was turtling in the deep gully and couldn't roll any further. "Van, help me!"

He took a hold of my feet and practically tossed me off the bag. I rolled off the side and straight onto the floor with a soft thump.

Luckily, my hand was still covering my vagina and successfully catching the stray fluids as I continued to laugh.

I felt something standing over me and opened my eyes.

"What?" I giggled.

Evander held out his hand for me, and I took it…with the wrong hand.

"Jesus fucking Christ."

"You still love me, Van?"

He pulled me in tight to him, uncaring about all the fluids that were now making our bodies slip against each other.

"There is one thing on this Earth that has the power to destroy me. That's you," he declared. "I love you, and I can't imagine a life without you. There's not a single moment that goes by throughout the day that I don't think about you. So yes, I love you. It doesn't matter if you break my heart for all to see…I'll love you forever and always."

My lip trembled as tears started to trail out of my eyes.

"And the baby you're carrying?" He ran the backs of his fingers up the side of my barely there bump. "My life."

I drew in a shaky breath.

"I love you, too, Van," I told him. "So much that I don't even have the words to describe it."

He winked and then lifted me into his arms once again.

"Now, let's go shower and do it all over again."

I started to giggle.

"As long as it's not in my Lovesac, I'll do just about anything."

And I forever would.

ABOUT THE AUTHOR

Lani Lynn Vale is married to the love of her life that she met in high school. She fell in love with him because he was wearing baseball pants. Ten years later they have three perfectly crazy children and a cat named Demon who likes to wake her up at ungodly times in the night. They live in the greatest state in the world, Texas. She writes contemporary and romantic suspense, and has a love for all things romance. You can find Lani in front of her computer writing away in her fictional characters' world...that is until her husband and kids demand sustenance in the form of food and drink.

Made in the USA
Middletown, DE
29 September 2017